The
Shy Stegosaurus
of
Indian Springs

By Evelyn Sibley Lampman

The Bounces of Cynthiann'

Captain Apple's Ghost

The City Under the Back Steps

Crazy Creek

Elder Brother

Navaho Sister

Rock Hounds

Rusty's Space Ship

The Shy Stegosaurus of Indian Springs

The Shy Stegosaurus of Cricket Creek

Special Year

Treasure Mountain

Tree Wagon

Witch Doctor's Son

ILLUSTRATED BY PAUL GALDONE

The
Shy Stegosaurus
of
Indian Springs

BY EVELYN (SIBLEY) LAMPMAN

DOUBLEDAY & COMPANY, INC.
GARDEN CITY, NEW YORK

The
Shy Stegosaurus
of
Indian Springs

CHAPTER ONE

"Lard and flour and salt."
On gnarled brown fingers Grandfather counted off the items which Huck must purchase at the agency store. "And oil for the lamp."

"And a sweet?" coaxed Huck hopefully.

Old Opalo's gray braids flapped from side to side with the motion of his head.

"We can do without a sweet. The other things we must have. Salt to season fish and the rabbits and squirrels. Lard, because it has been long since we had bear or venison to render our own fat. Flour, because it is not fitting that the medicine man or his great-grandson, Weewino, should stoop to the squaw-work of grinding meal. Only the coal oil for the lamp is a luxury."

Huck smothered his disappointment. He should have known it was useless to ask. Except for fruits and berries, Grandfather didn't care for sweets, and here on the reservation even those were in limited supply.

Occasionally fruit was brought in to the agency store, but Grandfather seldom bought produce of the land. Many of the more progressive Indians had planted fruit trees, apples and peaches and cherries, on their individual farms, and in the irrigated flats at Simnasho they had plots of strawberries and raspberries and melons. But Grandfather's acreage was not irrigated, and even if it were, Huck doubted if Opalo would lower himself to the planting and tending of crops. He expected nature to do that for him, as she had for his forefathers.

In the spring he diligently dug roots—*loosh, koush,* and *piachee*—some of which he cooked fresh, others of which he dried and stored for later use. In late summer, when the scouts had returned from the mountains with the news that the *weewinos,* the huckleberries, were blue and ripe on the bushes, and after the proper ceremonies had been observed at He He Longhouse, Opalo scurried off with his toting baskets, eager as any squaw to gather his share. But from one season to another, he could forget sweets and live on fish and game.

Huck couldn't. Dessert with dinner was the one thing which made him glad that he attended the agency boarding school nine months out of twelve. Otherwise he would have much preferred spending all the year with his grandfather in this rough, unpainted shack, set on arid, rocky ground which supported only sagebrush and occasional juniper. Grandfather was often stern, of course, and he refused to speak English, using only his tribal Klickitat, which sometimes was a little difficult for Huck, since he heard it only three months out of the year, and Grandfather did have some queer ideas, but he was kind. He didn't laugh at Huck, as did most of the children at the agency school, and call him a "blanket Indian." And when Grandfather addressed him as Weewino, it didn't sound degrading as when Bob Catchum and Nappy Post called him Huckleberry, even though it meant the same thing.

Those two were the only ones who called him that. Everyone else, even his teachers, settled for Huck, which wasn't quite so bad.

By now Grandfather had finished counting out the money for the supplies from an old deerskin pouch, and he put the silver in Huck's hand.

"Buy yourself a sweet," he said gently. "I have given you extra for that."

"A candy bar?" cried Huck joyfully.

Opalo frowned slightly at the English words. There was no Klickitat translation, and Huck had spoken impulsively.

"Buy what you will," he said severely. "You are a good boy, Weewino. Go now. It is a long way, and Paint is old. He cannot gallop as he once did."

Although it was still early morning, the sun was already warm. It just cleared the flat crest of the rimrock cliff which rose a short distance behind the shack and ran on for a few miles like a great protecting wall. Because it was still in shadows, the cliff looked gray this morning, streaked with mauve and blue where the rock was cut in great slashes and gullies; later, when the sun had climbed a little higher, it would be brown and gold and orange. Nothing grew on the steep sloping sides, and nothing grew on the top, which was so flat that Huck could imagine someone slicing it neatly with a knife. But at the very foot the sagebrush began, scattered clumps which sometimes widened to sizable stands as big as a good-sized flower bed.

It was too bad you couldn't eat sagebrush, Huck thought as he crossed over to the corral. But nobody could. It wasn't good for anything except to keep the

land from blowing away. At school last year they had studied soil erosion, and maybe that was the reason why people just left sagebrush alone and didn't try to clear it out.

As he reached the fence, however, he saw that someone had been clearing sagebrush. Yesterday there had been a high stand of it just beside the gate, but now it was gone. Grandfather must have decided it was in the way and pulled it up. But how could it have been in the way? The gate swung back in the opposite direction. There must have been another reason why Grandfather hadn't wanted it there. Of course, it was his land and his sagebrush, and he was entitled to do with it as he pleased, but just the same Huck didn't like to think of him doing silly, futile things like digging up sagebrush.

Bob Catchum and Nappy Post said everyone thought that Old Opalo was crazy, that he ought to be put away. At the time, Huck had torn into them both, and one of the teachers had come running to separate them. He had been too proud to tell what had started the fight, and neither Bob nor Nappy admitted saying anything out of the way, so Huck didn't really know whether everyone thought that about his grandfather or whether Bob and Nappy were only teasing. But ever since he had been careful to conceal as many of the old man's oddities as he could from the rest of the reservation.

He slipped off the leather thong which held the sagging gate in place, and Paint started galloping toward him. Usually the cayuse stood quietly in one spot, hardly seeming to notice when Huck threw the blanket over his back, but today he could hardly wait to cross the corral. His eyes rolled, showing the whites, and he thrust his soft nose into Huck's hand, seeming to beg for reassurance.

"What's the matter with you?" demanded Huck in amazement.

Paint's eyes rolled again. He stood trembling while the blanket was thrown in place, and as soon as Huck had leaped on his back he raced out of the open gate, as though pursued by a swarm of bees. He did not reduce his speed until a good mile had been put between them and the corral, but by that time he was wheezing so hard he had to stop.

"What's got into you?" Huck was worried. "You want to kill yourself off?"

Paint's spotted sides were wet, and his eyes continued to roll, but apparently he, too, saw the need for pausing to rest. He stood quite still on the narrow, rutty road, and after a moment his head drooped low, as though he might be contemplating the saffron dust underfoot.

Huck jumped down. He couldn't imagine what had got into Paint to make him behave that way. Maybe he'd been dreaming and thought he was a skittish young stallion again. Maybe he'd grown tired of his solitary life in the corral and of his occasional chore of hauling Opalo in a wagon or Huck on his back to the agency store and home again. Perhaps this was his way of revolting, of proving to his masters that he was as good a horse as he had ever been and was worthy of a more exciting existence.

Poor old Paint! If that were so, it must be a big let-

6

down. He was so winded now that it would take him a good while before he could go on. There was nothing to do but wait.

Huck told himself that it was too bad that he hadn't thought to bring the washing. Paint had given out close by the hot spring which Opalo used for that purpose, on the rare occasions when he felt it was necessary to wash anything. In the summer months that Huck lived with his grandfather, he did a washing every week, for cleanliness was a virtue greatly stressed by the agency school. He always gathered up his own soiled garments and as many of Opalo's as he could persuade the old man to part with, carried them here, and washed them as he had seen the older squaws wash theirs in the many hot springs closer to the agency. He was grateful that this particular spring was on his grandfather's property and too far away for anyone to see him at this woman-work.

Yes, it was a shame that he hadn't brought the washing. His other pair of jeans was dirty, and so were both of his shirts. He hadn't owned a clean one to wear to the agency this morning and had been forced to put on the one which showed fewer stains. Perhaps there would be time to wash it now. It would dry quickly in the sun. He looked critically at Paint's still-heaving sides and decided there would be plenty of time.

The hot spring was off the road and concealed from view by a rocky spur which separated from the main cliff and fanned out in a crescent. There were many springs like it on the reservation, some, like this, erupting singly from the barren ground and others, like those closer to the agency, clustered in groups of five or six.

In cold weather they gave off clouds of white steam, but in the summer the water bubbled up clearly, scenting the air with a sharp tang of minerals. The ground on one side of the spring had been worn away, so that the water spilled over in a little stream, collecting below in a shallow pool. Eventually, it must have been absorbed by the thirsty ground, for the depth and size of the pool remained constantly the right size for a washtub.

Peeling off his shirt as he walked, Huck circled the spur of rocks which rose higher than his head and entered his private laundry. Then he stopped short, and his black eyes filled with suspicion as they observed the spring, the adjacent pool, and the surrounding area. Someone had been here since he had! Someone had been digging great holes in the hard, rocky ground. Why, one of them was as big as a wheelbarrow!

His heart sank as he stared at the pitted ground. It was Grandfather, of course. No one else ever came here. And even if they did, they certainly wouldn't dig holes in a place where there was nothing to find. He remembered the sagebrush which had disappeared from behind the corral fence. Even that made more sense than this. It was Grandfather's right to remove sagebrush if it offended him, and it was his right to dig holes. But why would he do it? Why would anyone in his right mind dig holes when there was no reason to do so?

Automatically he continued on to the pool, knelt down, and dipped his soiled shirt into the warm water. He rubbed it back and forth between his hands, and the minerals brightened the fabric, cleaning it of grime. As he worked, his mind worried over the problem of Grandfather's latest peculiarity.

Bob and Nappy couldn't be right. He refused to believe it. Grandfather was old and determined to cling to the ways of his forefathers, but he was all right. He was good and kind. Hadn't he understood that Huck had wanted some candy more than anything and given his permission and the money to buy some? He patiently tried to teach Huck everything he knew— how to make snares and traps, how to dress hides, how to recognize signs so you were never lost, no matter where you were. What did it matter if he sometimes talked with spirits Huck couldn't see or cooked little dabs of roots and bark and then poured them on the ground as an offering to forgotten gods? Grandfather wasn't crazy. He was smart. Smarter than lots of people who laughed at him. But why did he have to go around digging meaningless holes in the ground? Huck was glad that no one ever came out here to their farm, where they might see these gaping excavations.

When the shirt was clean, he stood up and wrung it out. It was necessary to leave the secluded area of the spring to find a juniper to serve as a clothesline, and today he went, as always, to the same bush.

The bush grew on a ledge overlooking what was, to Huck, a most fascinating view. The boundaries of the reservation ended here, and down below, in a flat area below the cliff, was a rustic summer resort. He could see a row of cabins; a large, white-painted building, which presented only its back, so he didn't know what it was used for; and a large, tiled swimming pool

9

filled with sky-blue water. On Saturdays and Sundays, the pool was always crowded with bathers in bright-colored suits, and the parking lot behind the white building was full of cars. During the week, there were few customers for the pool, which Huck considered strange, because he thought that the whole resort—especially the pool—was beautiful and that people who could frequent such a place must be very rich.

Every week, when he finished his washing, he spread it out on the juniper, then lay down on his stomach on the ledge to watch the bathers. They were all strangers to him, for the Indians on the reservation swam in the river and did not patronize the pool. But sometimes, if the guests were hardy enough to withstand the spartan cabins longer than a week, Huck began to recognize them.

For two weeks he had watched a boy and girl about his own age. He guessed that they were twins: they were so close to a size, and they seemed to enjoy each other's company. The boy wore blue trunks and the girl a blue suit, and they both had red hair. They were only fair swimmers, but they were always chasing one another around the pool and ducking each other underwater. It looked like fun. Huck wished he had a twin, or at least a brother.

He spread his dripping shirt carefully across the spiny juniper, then walked over to the ledge. There lay the pool, blue and sparkling in the morning sunlight, and for a moment he thought it was deserted. Then a small figure in blue bathing trunks popped out from under a beach umbrella which had been anchored in the gray facing about the pool. It was followed immediately by a second figure in a blue suit. For a moment the two stood staring directly up at him; then, surprisingly, they both began to wave.

Huck looked behind him. They were waving at him, for there was no one else around. A little shyly, he waved back. He hadn't known that all the time he had been spying on them, they had been watching him.

The boy stopped waving, and his arm made a circular motion. He was inviting Huck to come down, to join them at the pool. But Huck was too shy. Besides, he had to get Grandfather's supplies from the agency. He shook his head no, he couldn't come.

The distance was too far for voices to carry, but the twins understood. The boy stopped beckoning. He saw them speaking together; then both began a more involved pantomime. They were trying to tell him something, to give him a message. He couldn't understand, and he thrust out his hands helplessly to tell them so.

This time the girl did the pantomime alone. She motioned to herself and her brother. Then she pointed to one of the cabins. They were going there, but they weren't going to stay long, for by gestures she made him understand that they would return. Then they could climb the cliff and join him.

For a moment Huck was pleased. He would have liked to know this boy and girl, to talk with them. They seemed friendly, and it would be good to have a friend. He had none at the school. Although Nappy and Bob were the only ones who said it aloud, he knew that the others thought him strange. They avoided him whenever they could, left him out of everything. Perhaps it was because he was the great-grandson of a medicine man and no one believed in such things anymore.

Then he remembered those gaping holes around the hot spring. Anyone who saw them would ask questions.

He shook his head violently. By motions he tried to tell them that they mustn't come up here. The cliff was too steep, too dangerous. Besides, he wouldn't be here when they arrived. He had to go away. He had to go right now.

Without even stopping to make sure they understood, he turned and hurried off. He and Paint were halfway to the agency before he remembered that he had left his wet shirt on the juniper bush.

CHAPTER *TWO*

Huck left Paint
in the store parking lot next to Chief Charley White-water's new automobile. It was a beautiful car, bright red with lots of silver trimming, which sparkled in the sun, and with white leather upholstery. There were other cars in the lot, but Charley's was the finest, and Huck thought that was entirely proper, since he was the chief of the confederated tribes living on the reservation.

There were three major tribes in the Confederation —the Wascos, the Warm Springs, and the Paiutes— but there were also a dozen or so representatives of other tribes whose numbers had grown so small that, even in 1855 when the reservation was established, they could not fill one by themselves. The Klickitats, to which Huck and his grandfather belonged, were one of these.

The confederated tribes at Warm Springs had much in common, and they were distinctive for the way they had held onto their birthright and their people. Originally they had all owned horses; now they all owned timber, the sale of which provided the income for the individual members. In addition, they derived government funds from their tribal fishing rights at Celilo and from the fees charged to fishermen in the reservoir behind Pelton Dam and in the Warm Springs River.

13

The younger members were progressive. They farmed or worked in lumber, drove cars like Charley White-water's instead of riding horses, and their wives did their laundry in automatic machines instead of by hand in the mineral pools. But there were a few, like Opalo and Martha Whitewater, Charley's grandmother, who clung to the old ways, and when their shares of tribal money were paid, they simply stored it away in leather bags and doled it out as a concession to a civilization they resented. Huck didn't resent progress and civiliza-tion. He thought it was good, but he thought Grand-father Opalo was good, too, and he didn't intend to have anybody criticizing him.

When he rounded the side of the building and saw Bob Catchum and Nappy Post coming out the door, he almost stopped. Then he continued on, for it was too late. They had already seen him.

"Look who's here," yelled Bob, his black eyes glitter-ing with anticipation. "Old Huckleberry!"

"Yeah," said Nappy quickly. "Old Huckleberry Hound!"

They were eating ice-cream bars, which were melt-ing fast in the hot sun. Bob stopped to lick a streak of chocolate from his hand, then wiped his sticky fingers on his T-shirt.

"Where's your blanket, Huckleberry?" he demanded. "Old Trout wouldn't like it if he knew you were out without your blanket."

"My grandfather's name is Opalo," Huck reminded him angrily.

"That's what I said. Opalo means trout. I asked my grandma. She doesn't remember much of the lingo, but

14

she remembered that all right. Old Trout. And Huckleberry. What a pair!"

"Has Old Trout made any medicine lately?" jeered Nappy. "Called up a devil or something?"

That was too much. With burning face and clenched fists, Huck started up the step prepared to do battle. It didn't matter that there were two of them to his one or that they were both a year older than he. This time he would have it out. He would fight till he was dead if need be. They couldn't talk that way about his grandfather.

At that moment, the screen door opened and Charley Whitewater came out. He carried a big bag of groceries in his arms.

"Hey, fellows," he said reproachfully, looking at Bob and Nappy. "A bargain's a bargain. If I give you a lift to the swimming hole, you're supposed to help me carry groceries to the car. There's two more sacks still inside."

"Yes, sir," cried Bob.

"We will, Chief," echoed Nappy.

They turned and raced back inside the store. Charley Whitewater stood still, balancing his heavy brown bag and grinning down at the remaining boy on the steps.

"How are you, Huck?" he asked genially. "How's your grandfather?"

"Fine, sir." Some of the heat was beginning to fade from Huck's cheeks, but he was still angry. Chief Whitewater had spoiled it for now, but there would be another time. Bob and Nappy would have to be taught a lesson.

"You know, I worry about your grandfather," confessed the chief. "Not so much in the summer, when you're there, but in the winter, while you're in school. He's getting too old to be living out there all by himself."

"He likes it that way," Huck assured him quickly. "He wouldn't be happy anywhere else."

"But if something should happen . . . if he should hurt himself, maybe fall and break a bone . . . Your grandfather's no spring chicken, Huck. My grandmother's nearly ninety, and Opalo's older than she is."

"But he's very healthy. He's never sick."

"We'll have to see." Chief Whitewater sounded unconvinced. "We have to look after our own people, Huck. You know that."

"Yes, sir," said Huck weakly. He hoped Chief Whitewater would forget about it. If Grandfather insisted on digging holes and clearing sagebrush, it would be better done in secret.

Bob and Nappy hurried through the door bearing huge brown-paper sacks, and the chief good-naturedly motioned them to precede him down the steps.

"See you, Huck." He nodded.

Huck went on inside, feeling more miserable than ever. Now he had a new problem to worry about. Chief Whitewater meant well, but he mustn't take Grandfather away from his own house and his own land.

Lily Franchere had a summer job helping out in the store, and she called to him from behind the counter.

"Hello, Huck. I haven't seen you since school was out."

Huck had always thought Lily ought to be in the movies. It usually made him feel good just to look at

16

her, because she was so pretty, but today he was so angry with Bob and Nappy and so upset by Chief Whitewater's suggestion that Grandfather was too old to live alone that he hardly noticed her.

"Is something wrong?" she asked anxiously when he only nodded at her greeting.

"No," he told her quickly. "I'm just in a hurry. I've got to get back home."

He enumerated the items on Opalo's list, and Lily fetched them from the shelves and placed them in two leather bags connected by a rope, so that they would hang across Paint's back. When they had distributed salt and flour, coal oil, and lard so they would balance properly, Huck remembered the candy bar Grandfather had said he could buy. He went over to the counter and tried to make up his mind.

"Do you want the six-cent kind or the ten-cent?" Lily smiled.

Huck hesitated. Grandfather hadn't said. He had left it up to him. He could buy whatever he wanted, a bar, or ice cream, or even a bottle of pop.

"I don't know. I thought I wanted a chocolate bar. Now I don't know."

"It is hot for chocolate," agreed Lily. "It's melting in the wrappers. I wish the weather would cool off a little. They're talking about closing down the woods because of the fire hazard, and the farmers' crops are drying up. It's hurting us, too. We got that bunch of bananas over there just last Monday, and they were pretty green. But look how they've all ripened! We had to put a special price on them, ten cents a pound, hoping people will buy them before they spoil."

Huck's eyes followed her pointing finger. From the ceiling hung a stalk of golden-yellow bananas, and he felt his mouth begin to water. He hadn't had a banana for months, and they were his favorite fruit. Probably they were everyone's favorite. They might even be Grandfather's, once he tasted them. Huck doubted very much if he ever had. Opalo wouldn't touch candy, but he never turned up his nose at fruit. Huck made up his mind instantly.

"How many bananas do you get for ten cents?"

"Depends on the size." Lily crossed the room and stood by the long, irregularly shaped cluster. "Maybe two this size. Maybe three smaller ones."

"I'll take two big ones." Huck's black eyes shone. That would be one for himself and one for Opalo, and it wouldn't cost anymore than a single candy bar. It would be his present to Grandfather.

Lily selected the two largest bananas on the stalk and cut them off with a little knife. She did not put them on the scales but placed one in each of the two leather bags.

"Be careful," she advised. "Don't mash them. They're very ripe."

"I won't. I'll keep them on the very top and see that there's nothing up against them," he promised.

Paint seemed to have recovered completely from his earlier inclinations to gallop. He plodded slowly, wearily, back down the little-used wagon road to Opalo's acreage, pausing often to rest. From time to time, Huck dismounted and walked because it seemed cruel to make the tired old cayuse carry additional weight.

He could smell the bananas even through the leather

bags, and he worried lest they ripen so much on the way home that they would be unfit to eat. Several times he considered eating his own before he arrived, particularly since he was getting very hungry. It had been a long time since breakfast. At last he couldn't stand it any longer. He took it out of the bag just as they reached the spot next to the hot spring where they had rested that morning.

Simultaneously Paint halted once more, signifying that he needed to rest, and Huck slid down. He might just as well get his shirt from the juniper bush so long as he was here.

For the second time that day he circled the rocks and stood surveying the hot spring and pool, encircled by pitted, rocky ground. He couldn't imagine how an old man like Grandfather could have made such holes and gashes. It looked as though someone had been using a bulldozer.

He leaned against a huge boulder while he thought about it, carefully breaking open the top of the banana and peeling down the golden skin. It looked like a cream-colored candle rising from the peelings, and one moment he was looking at it there in his hand and the next instant it was gone. The banana had disappeared, skin and all, into a parrotlike beak which had shot out from the side of the boulder and now snapped shut with a satisfied click.

Huck clung to the rock, frozen with terror. His eyes followed up from the beak and encountered a pair of beady, black eyes, which stared back at him unblinkingly. The beak and the eyes were part of a round head, only a little above his own. But, despite the snapping beak, the head was not nearly so frightening as the body to which it belonged. That towered up and up, developing into proportions larger than those of an elephant. It was covered with hard, leathery skin in mottled shades of brown and gray, tan and yellow and orange, with even a little purple here and there.

As Huck stared, the creature shifted about, and it was as though part of the rocky cliff was moving. The creature's coloring was exactly the same as the cliff's, and its irregular shape blended so perfectly with the jagged rocks that Huck had to look twice to see where one left off and the other began. It stood on four ponderous legs, as big as the largest tree trunks he had ever seen, and its huge padded feet were the size of dishpans. Its front legs were much shorter than its back

legs, which gave it a curious, humped-up appearance. Along its backbone ran a row of triangular shields two feet high, and behind trailed a formidable tail ten feet long, terminating in four wicked spikes, each one of which was almost as tall and as big as Huck himself. What was even worse, the tail moved constantly back and forth in what seemed to be a truly menacing gesture.

Huck closed his eyes to shut out the frightful sight, and to his amazement he heard a gentle voice speaking in perfect English.

"Delicious! Delectable! Exactly as I remembered them! Oh, for the days of my youth, when bananas grew here in abundance. They were my favorite food! Forgive me for being grabby, but when I smelled them

again, after all these years, I just couldn't restrain myself."

Huck opened his eyes. There was no one there but himself and the monster. The words were issuing from the beaklike mouth.

Forgetting those gigantic feet which could crush him underfoot and the spiked tail which could tear him to bits, Huck gave a shriek of terror. Then he turned and dashed around the sheltering boulder, away from the area of the hot spring and the frightful monster who was able to speak like a man.

CHAPTER *THREE*

OPALO SWALLOWED
the last tip of banana and reluctantly threw down the peeling.

"Good! Perhaps we should plant some of this fruit. If it is not too much work," he added cautiously.

"Bananas don't grow here, Grandfather," explained Huck. "They aren't like apples and peaches. They only grow where it's hot."

"It is hot." Opalo wiped perspiration from his face with his ragged shirt sleeve and looked at his grandson severely.

"But it gets cold in the winter. It freezes, and the snow is thick for months. Where bananas grow, it's hot all the year around."

Opalo had never heard of such a climate. His scornful eyes doubted if it existed anywhere.

"Grandfather, did you ever see a monster?" Huck changed the subject to the one he had been waiting to introduce ever since his return home. He had been too nervous before to talk about his experience at the spring. It had seemed wiser to put it from his mind, so far as he was able, and try to return to normal before recalling his recent fright.

"Many times," nodded Opalo solemnly. "I am a medicine man. I have visions. Often they are of monsters."

"But outside of a vision," insisted Huck. "Did you ever really see one?"

Opalo looked at him without answering, and Huck realized that the old man had no intention of doing so. Perhaps he considered the question impertinent. He tried again.

"Did one of the monsters you saw in a vision ever talk to you?"

"They speak by signs," his grandfather admitted grudgingly. "But I have been trained to read those signs, so I know the meaning of their visits. There are not many of us left who know these things."

"But couldn't they speak if they wanted to? If they appeared to someone who didn't know the signs? Who wasn't a medicine man?"

"They would never do so," scoffed Opalo. "They know the sorry state to which our people have sunk. They appear less and less, only to the old ones such as I. When we are gone, there will be no more visions and our people must suffer the consequences."

"But just suppose they did?" Huck persisted doggedly. "Suppose *I* saw one of those monsters? And suppose it talked to me?"

Opalo raised himself from the sagging step where he had been sitting. He glared down angrily at his great-grandson.

"You are as bad as the others," he scolded. "You have picked up their wicked, unbelieving ways. Someday you will be sorry. But then it will be too late."

He stalked indignantly toward the open doorway of the shack, pausing only long enough to shout an order over his shoulder.

"Tomorrow you will go again to the agency. Bring back more of that yellow fruit which grows only in a land which has no snow."

Huck sighed. Sometimes his grandfather was very hard to understand. Perhaps, by tomorrow, his grandfather would be in a mellower mood and would be willing to discuss monsters.

Lately Opalo had been growing more and more absentminded. He frequently gave orders one day and by the next morning forgot all about them. But he did not forget about the bananas. As soon as they had finished their breakfast of trout and cakes baked from the flour which Huck had carried home from the store, he brought out the leather bag, heavy with money. It was all silver, for the old man had no faith in paper currency and would never accept it, even from the Tribal Council, as his share of the fishing rights.

"Go for the yellow fruit," he ordered. "This time, bring more than one."

Huck hesitated.

"What are you going to do today, Grandfather?"

For the first time, he was afraid to go away and leave Opalo alone. What if the monster should come here from the hot spring? The medicine man would think he was having a vision. He might stand still, waiting for signs which wouldn't come, and the creature might club him with that formidable spiked tail or crush him underfoot with one of those gigantic feet. For Huck was very sure the monster was no vision. It was alive, a terrifying creature of flesh and blood, and probably only Huck's own speedy heels had saved him from a terrible death.

He had been too tired to stay awake last night worrying about it, but his sleep had been filled with dreams in which the monster had chased him from one rimrock ledge to another, and he had only managed to elude capture by waking up in the nick of time.

"I may sleep a little." Opalo yawned hugely.

"Better lock the door," advised Huck in a relieved tone. "You wouldn't want anyone walking in while you were asleep."

Opalo stared at him without speaking. There was no need to lock the door, his eyes reminded his grandson. The possibility of anyone's walking into the house was very remote. No outsiders came to these acres anymore. Why should they?

When Huck went outside, he could guess why his grandfather was tired this morning. A sizable stand of sagebrush in the field close to the house had been completely cleared out. It had been there when they went to bed; Huck was sure of that. Opalo must have arisen quietly during the night and disposed of it. For a moment he considered questioning the old man about his motives; then he decided against it. Opalo didn't like questions and probably wouldn't answer.

Paint took his usual leisurely gait this morning, but as they neared the rocks which hid the mineral spring from the road Huck kicked him into a trot. Never again would he linger around that place. He could no longer use the pool as a washtub, either, or watch the people swimming in the resort pool below. It wouldn't be safe.

Then he thought once more of his grandfather. Opalo's washings were rare, but he did go to the spring once in a while. Either he would have to be stopped or the monster must be removed. That, of course, was the sensible thing to do. Huck doubted that he himself was capable of such action, but the Tribal Council could take care of it. He was surprised at himself for not having thought of it before. All he had to do was report the presence of the monster to Chief Whitewater. He would do the rest.

The Whitewater farm was ten miles on the other side of the agency, too far for such an old horse as Paint to go and return in the same day. But Huck was sure that the chief made daily trips into the agency. Yesterday their visits had coincided; he hoped that they would today. But when he clucked Paint into the parking lot beside the store, there was no shiny red automobile standing there; there was only the conservative gray coupé which belonged to the agency doctor.

When Huck went inside, Lily Franchere was putting Dr. Mercer's purchase, a quarter's worth of horehound candy, into a sack. The doctor held out the open bag, an invitation for Huck to help himself.

"No, thank you," said Huck politely. It was the only kind of candy he didn't like.

"Don't blame you," said Dr. Mercer cheerfully. "I can't stand the taste of it myself, but Old Martha Whitewater likes it. I always take her some when I stop by to see Charley."

"Are you going out to the Whitewaters'?" Huck could hardly believe his luck. Ten miles was nothing in a car, and Paint would rest patiently in the parking lot until he returned.

The doctor nodded. "I have some papers for Charley to sign. Why?"

"Could I go with you, please? I have to talk to the chief. It's very important."

"Why, sure," agreed Dr. Mercer good-naturedly. "Glad to have company."

Huck ordered his bananas first, and Lily promised to pick out nice ones and put them away until he returned. Then he followed the doctor outside and climbed into the coupé beside him.

Dr. Mercer backed out of the lot and onto the road. Beyond the store, the white-painted government buildings glistened in the sun, and the lawns surrounding them were lushly green, for there was water on this portion of the reservation. Some children were playing on the slide in back of the school, and their voices carried shrilly in the warm air.

Huck wondered again, as he had so many times before, when individuals chose their own land from the 536,000 acres on the reservation, why his great-great-grandfather had selected the dry, barren northern acres over this fertile valley on the timbered mountain slopes. Chief Whitewater's great-grandparents had been more discerning. His land lay along the banks of the Warm Springs River, and as Dr. Mercer turned his car off the highway and onto the graveled country road, Huck could hear the water rippling over rocks and boulders behind the thick tangle of bushes on the bank.

"It's a good day to go swimming," observed Dr. Mercer, whose ears had also caught the sound of water.

"Yes, it is," agreed Huck politely.

"My business won't take long, but I could probably spare a half hour if you want to take a dip when we get there."

"When Chief Whitewater hears my news, there will not be time," said Huck. "He'll want to do something about it right away, and he will need me as a guide."

"I guess it's pretty important news that you bring him," suggested Dr. Mercer.

"Yes," said Huck briefly.

Chief Whitewater's farm, like his automobile, was a model to inspire the rest of the reservation. His house and barns were not new, but they were in perfect repair and freshly painted. A picket fence encircled the yard, and beyond the house was a vegetable garden, with beans growing on poles thrust into the ground like the ribs of tepees, young corn not yet ripe enough to tassel, and heads of cabbage and kale.

The chief came out of the barn as Dr. Mercer's car pulled into the driveway, and he crossed the yard to greet them.

"Doc, glad to see you," he called cheerfully. "Hello, Huck."

"I brought those papers for you to sign, Charley," said Dr. Mercer, shutting off the engine and opening the car door. "And Huck here has some news he says is mighty important."

"Something about your grandfather, Huck?" asked Chief Whitewater quickly. "He's not sick?"

"Oh no. Nothing like that. It's not about Grandfather at all. But it's something you should know about."

"Oh." As soon as he heard that the news did not concern Opalo, Chief Whitewater appeared to lose interest. He wiped his face with a handkerchief which he pulled from a back pocket. "Let's go up to the house. Marie keeps the shades pulled down. Makes you think it's cooler, anyway."

Chief Whitewater and Dr. Mercer started off, and Huck tagged along behind. Once they heard his news, once they learned that there was a monster loose on the reservation, they wouldn't take it so calmly. He could picture their horror and astonishment when they heard of the danger that threatened—and the gratitude which would finally be his for having warned them in time.

An old woman was sitting on the sunny front porch, huddled in a shawl. She looked at them with sharp, bright eyes from an incredibly wrinkled face.

"Hello, Martha," called Dr. Mercer genially. "Nice to see you. I've brought you a present."

He held out the sack of candy. A thin, clawlike hand shot out from the shawl to take it from him, and she mumbled something in the Indian tongue.

"Grandmother says thank you. You're very kind to remember her as you do," said Chief Whitewater promptly.

Huck smothered a smile, for it wasn't what she had said at all. She had muttered, "Then give it to me, white man. Then go away."

"Good afternoon, Grandmother-of-the-Chief," said Huck, using the Klickitat tongue with which he spoke to his own grandfather. Although Martha Whitewater was a Warm Springs, there was enough similarity in the languages so that she could understand.

The bright old eyes regarded him closely between the overhanging layers of skin.

"You are Opalo's grandson," she said finally. "I have seen you at the festivals, at the Suppul-wit, the Root Festival in the spring, and the Huckleberry Festival in late summer."

"Yes, Grandmother. I am Weewino, great-grandson of Opalo, once medicine man of the Klickitats."

"You are a polite boy," she decided, and held out the bag of candy. "Sit down on the step and talk with me."

Huck hesitated. His business with the chief was urgent, but the chief would not even listen until he had finished signing Dr. Mercer's papers. And it was unthinkable to be rude. He sat down on the step beside her and reluctantly accepted one of the candies from the sack.

"How is your grandfather?" asked Martha. "How does he spend his time?"

"He is well, although he is old and cannot walk so far as he once did. He traps, and sometimes he rides to Beaver Creek and fishes. He can no longer climb the cliff to fish in the Warm Springs. He gathers roots in the spring and dries them——"

"And he will go to the mountains for huckleberries when it is time," she interrupted. "I, too, cannot walk as I once did. But I will walk to the mountains for the huckleberries when it is time. Old we may be, and slower than we once were, Opalo and I, but we will never give up the old ways."

Perhaps, thought Huck quickly, here was a friend who might intercede for his grandfather. Martha would understand Opalo's need to stay on his own acres.

"Your grandson, the chief, thinks my grandfather is getting too old to live by himself," he said slyly. "He thinks he should be taken from his land and made to live with someone else."

"You are a big boy," Martha told him sternly. "Why do you not live with your grandfather?"

"I do, in the summer. But in the winter I go to the boarding school."

"Then you must stop going to school," decided Martha. "What good is it? Your grandfather did not go to school. I did not go to school. My grandson went to school, and the others who chose him chief went there. They said it was a place to learn. Instead it was a place to forget. My grandson has even forgotten the language of his fathers. He remembers only that of the white man. I do not like schools. The mighty Sim-tus-tus, the greatest hero our people have ever known, did not go to school. And there was never so great a scout as he. Even the white soldiers said he was the greatest scout in all the West. They called him Pipsher Sim-tus-tus. They paid him much trade goods and many horses to scout for them against the Paiutes and the Bannocks and the Modocs. When the white men put our people on this reservation, Sim-tus-tus showed them where mistakes had been made on their papers. He showed them where markers had been changed to cheat the Indians. And because of him, many acres, which had been stolen, were returned to our people. Then he told the Tribal Council never to sell its land, and we have not. No white man can buy it from us, though they try. Now they tell me they have named a lake for him, for Sim-tus-tus . . ."

Her voice faded away. Huck looked up startled and saw that she was staring across the yard, her bright eyes dulled with memories as they sought the past. She had completely forgotten that he was there, so he arose quietly and went into the house.

Chief Whitewater had just finished signing the papers

as Huck walked into the living room. It was such a splendid room that, for a moment, he almost forgot what he had come for and stood staring about him. There were a davenport and matching chair, upholstered in blue, with lace doilies over the arms and at the spots where anyone might rest his head. There were two brown wooden chairs with cushioned seats, a TV set on a small table, and a second table which held a vase filled with pink roses. There were pink roses on the carpet, too, and starched curtains at the windows. Through the open doorway leading to the dining room and kitchen beyond came a delectable odor of baking cookies and the sound of Marie Whitewater's voice, singing as she washed up the dishes.

"Come in, Huck," invited the chief. "Have a chair. We've finished up here, and now you can tell me what's on your mind."

Huck sat down in one of the cushioned chairs, wondering exactly how to begin. He ought to lead up to the subject gradually, for it would be a great shock. But he didn't know how to do so, so he just blurted it out.

"Chief, I saw a monster. As big as a chicken house. And it's got a tail with spikes on it this long. It's up at the hot spring on Grandfather's land, and I want you to come and kill it before it kills us."

For a moment both men stared at him without speaking. Then the chief again pulled out his handkerchief and wiped his brown, damp face.

"Huck, it's just too hot to be playing games," he objected. "I don't mind being kidded, but——"

"I'm not kidding," interrupted Huck. "It's there. I

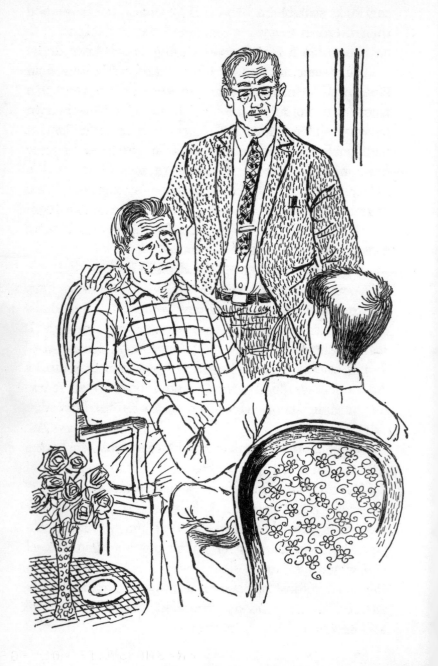

saw it. It snatched a banana right out of my hand, and then it talked to me."

"What did it say to you?" asked Dr. Mercer dryly.

"Why, something about it's having been a long time since it had a banana." Huck screwed his forehead into wrinkles trying to remember. He had given no thought to what the creature had said; he knew only how it had looked. "I think it said that bananas used to grow here and that they were its favorite food."

"Either you're making this up," declared Chief Whitewater angrily, "or you're sick. Which is it, Doc?"

"I don't think he's sick," said Dr. Mercer. "It's more likely a highly developed imagination."

"No, it isn't. I saw it! It was a monster!" cried Huck.

"What did it look like?" asked the doctor calmly. "Try to describe it for us, Huck."

"It was big. Huge. Its head wasn't so big, though. It was small for the rest of him, and it hung down sort of low. And it had great, huge legs, like barrels, only the front ones were shorter than the back ones. And it was sort of humped up, and along its back were two rows of things that stood up like horns, only they were flat. And its tail was long, and it had four great big spikes on the end."

"Has your grandfather been telling you stories, Huck?" asked the chief sharply. "Has he been scaring you with old witch doctors' stories?"

"Oh no, sir. Grandfather didn't see it at all. Just me."

"I don't think Old Opalo would be likely to recognize the creature he's just described, Charley," chuckled Dr. Mercer. "I think Huck read about it himself in a book and imagined that he saw one."

"What's that?" asked the chief suspiciously.

"A dinosaur," declared the doctor. "That's what he's described, all right. Huck's read about them, in school probably. And maybe he fell asleep and dreamed about them. When he woke up, the dream was so real he believed it."

"Oh," said the chief in a relieved tone. "Is that it, Huck?"

"No, sir," declared Huck stubbornly. "I really saw it."

"You just thought you did," Dr. Mercer told him positively. "The last dinosaur died 60,000,000 years ago."

"How about some iced tea and fresh cookies?" asked Marie Whitewater from the doorway. "Huck, do you want to take the tray and pass them around for me?"

Huck stood up and did as he was asked. The conversation about monsters was at an end, and he knew it. But the subject wasn't settled in his own mind. Whether he had met a dinosaur he didn't know, but he was positive that he hadn't dreamed that encounter at the hot spring.

CHAPTER *FOUR*

WHEN HUCK ARRIVED HOME, he found that his grandfather had already begun preparations for their evening meal. He maintained a half dozen traps within easy walking distance of the house, and now a rabbit was boiling on top of the rusty iron stove. The fire made the small room unbearably hot, but Opalo did not notice. He was in good spirits, especially when he saw the dozen overripe bananas which his grandson had brought.

"We will eat one now," he decided. "To stay our hunger while the rabbit cooks."

"I'll save mine till later," Huck told him.

The heat of the room, the smell of boiling rabbit, and the roots which Opalo had thrown into the pot made him feel ill. Ever since Chief Whitewater and Dr. Mercer had declared that there was no such thing as a monster and had accused Huck of making up the story, his stomach had been churning round and round. Was it possible that they were right? Could he have dreamed the whole thing?

Opalo peeled back the banana skin quickly and devoured the fruit in great, snapping bites. It was nice that his grandfather still had his teeth, Huck thought, remembering that when Martha Whitewater had talked, he had glimpsed bare gums. Opalo's teeth were no longer white, and they were worn short, but every one was still in place. However, his eyesight was no longer as clear as it had been.

"You took a long time at the store," he chided, finishing off the last of the banana and looking at his grandson searchingly. "You were late coming home."

"I went out to Chief Whitewater's with Dr. Mercer," explained Huck. "I saw his grandmother. She asked about you. She says she is going huckleberrying again this year."

"Of course she will go." Opalo spoke irritably. "She is the first of the twelve scouts chosen by the Council to say when the huckleberries are ripe. The appointment is not made lightly, and the position is held for life. Martha is the oldest of the twelve squaws, and likely the only one to know her business. Left to themselves, the other eleven would doubtless get into their fast automobiles and drive to the mountains. The only way they could tell when the berries are ripe would be to squeeze them."

"How can Martha tell?" asked Huck meekly.

"She will examine the pods of the wild rose and of the chokecherry. When they are of a proper ripeness, so will the huckleberries be ripe. Then we will gather in the old way to give thanks to the Great Spirit for his bounty, and after that our people may eat of the fruit."

There was something in the old man's tone which made Huck look at him in surprise. His grandfather was not an imposing man. He was small and thin, and his gray hair hung over his shoulders in two greasy braids. He wore a pair of dirty trousers far too large for him, held up at the waist by a strand of heavy cord, and a ragged dark shirt, open at the throat. But as he spoke of the ancient festival and the ceremonies surrounding it, he seemed to grow larger, to acquire a serene and unaccustomed dignity.

A moment later, he became his former self as he reached one thin arm behind to scratch viciously at his shoulder blade.

"Tomorrow I go to the spring," he announced. "There are lice in my blanket. They bite me at night. It must be washed clean."

"I'll go, Grandfather," cried Huck hastily. Opalo was an old man. He couldn't run fast. If there really was a monster at the spring, it wouldn't be safe for him to go there. "I have to go to the spring anyway. Yesterday I left my other shirt there."

"Very well." Opalo stood up and walked over to the stove, sniffing at the bubbling pot. "It is more seemly for a boy to do woman's work than it is for a medicine man."

Huck slept fitfully that night. Again he kept dreaming that the monster was chasing him, and when he tried to run away, Chief Whitewater and Dr. Mercer kept blocking his path, trying to make him go back. He woke up from the same dream time after time, and the waking was even harder than being asleep, because he knew that tomorrow he would either have to face this danger or confess his fear to Opalo. Opalo wouldn't believe him either, since Huck was not a medicine man and monsters appeared only to them in visions, but when he realized that Huck was really frightened, he might insist on accompanying him to the spring. And he couldn't do that. Opalo was too old; his legs were too shaky to run. Of course, he did have a gun. It was standing in the corner behind the door, and if the monster were real, Opalo could shoot it. But why, Huck asked himself, did he have to bring his grandfather into it at all? Why didn't he just take the gun and use it himself?

The more he thought about it, the more he liked the idea. It would be a fine thing to kill a monster. Once it was dead, he could insist on Chief Whitewater's and Dr. Mercer's coming to the spot and inspecting the body. They wouldn't laugh then or tell him he was imagining things. The decision made him feel much better, and he finally fell into a dreamless sleep to the accompaniment of his grandfather's snores from the next room.

His resolve was still firm the following morning. He slipped the gun outside the door while Opalo was dishing up the remains of the rabbit stew for their breakfast. After that he began collecting the laundry, the two blankets from his grandfather's bed, and his own soiled clothing. Everything, including the gun, could be wrapped in the blankets. It would make an oddly shaped bundle, but perhaps, with Opalo's failing eyesight, he wouldn't notice and ask questions.

Finally, Opalo slipped out of his shirt and trousers and gave them to his grandson. Outside of his tribal paraphernalia, they were the only garments he owned, but since it promised to be hot and they never had visitors, he could get along without them for a day.

Huck took one of the remaining bananas, now quite brown and soft, and, with his curiously shaped bundle of laundry, started down the old wagon road. It was almost two miles to the spring, but he had already decided not to take Paint. Like Opalo, the cayuse was very old, and Huck would have never forgiven himself if anything happened.

As he walked, he had his first misgivings. What if the gun wouldn't fire? He had made sure that it was loaded, but it hadn't been used for years. Opalo preferred trapping game to shooting it. It was cheaper, and, besides, it was the old way of his people. Even if it did fire, perhaps the shot wouldn't penetrate the monster's skin. It had looked very hard and tough. But, then, people shot elephants, and their skin must be thick, too.

The most dangerous part of the mission, he had already decided, was that he might be caught unaware. He hadn't seen the monster coming before. It had just stepped out from some crevice in the rocks. Suppose it pounced on him before he had a chance to raise his weapon? That's why he had brought the banana. His grandfather thought Huck intended to eat it himself, but he meant to use it for bait. He would approach only as far as the first boulder, throw the banana into the circle of stones next to the spring, and when the monster stepped out of its hiding place, he would shoot it. If something went wrong, he would run.

It seemed a very good plan. Huck didn't see how he could improve upon it, but by the time he reached the rocky spur of the cliff which concealed the spring, he was shaking a little. He put down his blanket-wrapped bundle and took out the gun, moving carefully in order not to make a sound. Then he flattened himself against

41

the edge of the boulder, sliding his body along against the rock until he was far enough around to see the rough ground, the spring, and the pool.

So far as he could determine, the area was empty. The sun had not yet climbed high enough to peer over the edge of the cliff, so the little cavern was in shadows, but he seemed to be quite alone. He could hear the soft murmurs of the water as it spilled from the spring and trickled down into the pool. He could smell the faint tang of minerals above the almost sweetish-sick odor of the overripe banana in his hand. But he could see no monster.

He flung the banana from him as far as he could. It bounced once before settling into one of the holes which had been dug into the ground around the spring. Huck held his breath, waiting. Then he heard a voice speaking to him, a mild voice, which echoed slightly against the rocky walls.

"You have come again. I am very glad you did. The last time you left before I could apologize for my rudeness in taking your fruit or even thank you for it."

Huck's eyes shifted wildly around the rocky enclosure. He could see no one.

"You and I have much in common, you know," continued the voice. "We're both shy. I've watched you come here for some time. You are always alone. It is probably because you're too shy to make friends. And so am I. But when you came, bringing my favorite fruit, I just couldn't help myself. My instinct told me to take it, and so I did. Then you were too shy to wait for my thanks, so you ran away. Now you come bringing me more fruit. You would like to be friends."

42

Huck swallowed. Monsters didn't talk that way. At least he didn't think they did.

"Now my instinct is divided," confessed the voice, which, because of the echo, seemed to come simultaneously from all three sides of the rocky enclosure. "It tells me to accept your latest gift, but it also tells me that, if I do, you will run away again. And I don't want you to run away."

"Why not?" Huck's voice came out in an odd croak.

"Because I am lonely. Just as you are. Lonely and shy."

"Are you sure it's not because you want to eat me up?" He was growing a little bolder now.

"Are you trying to spoil our friendship before it begins?" The echoing voice crackled with sharpness. "This is the second time in my life that I've been accused of that, and it's most upsetting. The last time, I had to sharpen my tail for a whole night before I calmed down. Your brain must be even smaller than mine if you don't know that I am a vegetarian."

"I'm sorry." Huck spoke quickly, for there seemed to be real hurt in the tone. "But I can't see you, and it's hard to talk to somebody you aren't looking at. You're hiding somewhere in the rocks, and I don't really know who I'm talking to."

"That's true," agreed the voice, somewhat mollified. "If I step out so you can see me, will you promise to stay and chat awhile?"

"You're sure you wouldn't hurt me?"

"I have never hurt a friend," announced the voice in an aggrieved tone, and the next moment the creature stepped out from against the rocky cliff where it had been standing.

43

It was exactly as Huck remembered it, the small, low-hung head; the rapidly rising back, surmounted by spiny shields; the long tail, which wagged constantly from side to side, like a dog's, and which ended in four ferocious-looking spikes.

For a moment Huck pushed back against the boulder; then, because he knew it was expected of him, he stepped forward a few inches. He still clutched his gun, the trigger close to his finger.

"Try not to be shy," coaxed the creature. "Although I know that you cannot help it. What is your name?"

"Huck."

"I have never heard that name before." The great tail stopped wagging for a moment while the creature

seemed to consider. Then it continued. "You may call me George. Of course, I don't need to tell you that I am a stegosaurus. I understand that human mammals are very interested in us. They admire us so much that they even collect our footprints in old rocks. Some of them are ghoulish enough to hunt for our bones, which I consider a most disgraceful thing to do."

Huck did not know what a stegosaurus was. He didn't believe they had studied about them in school.

"You are dreadfully big," he admitted.

"Not at all," objected George. "It is you who are dreadfully small. Most mammals are of insignificant size. Fifteen feet long, not counting my tail, which is another ten, is average size. Tyrannosaurus was fifty feet tall,

Brontosaurus was seventy, while Diplodocus, poor thing, was eighty-seven feet from his snout to his tail tip. That is really too large. It's why he had to spend most of the time in the water to help support his weight. He was far too heavy to stand very long on his legs."

Huck had never heard any of those names, but he remembered what Dr. Mercer had said.

"Are you related to the dinosaurs?" he asked.

"I *am* a dinosaur," answered George promptly. "Tyrannosaurus, Brontosaurus, Allosaurus—all of us are dinosaurs. Goodness me, you really must have a small brain not to know that!"

"Well——"

"Oh, don't apologize," interrupted the stegosaurus kindly. "A small brain must be another thing we have in common, like our shyness. It brings us closer together. You see, I have a small brain, too. You wouldn't believe it, because I've come to use my instinct in its place, but my brain is no larger than a nut. You, poor dear, must have one even smaller than that. But don't be discouraged. Instinct will serve you just as well."

Huck tried to cover his rising indignation at this criticism of his brain. It would be just as well not to quarrel with anything quite so large as a stegosaurus.

"If you're a real dinosaur," he asked, "how come you're still alive? Dr. Mercer says there haven't been any dinosaurs for 60,000,000 years."

"He's wrong," declared George positively. "For here am I. Of course, I can't tell you how I happen to be here. If I had a brain, perhaps I could explain it. But this is one instance in which instinct will not serve."

"And how come you can talk?" persisted Huck.

"That is another thing instinct cannot explain," admitted the stegosaurus reluctantly. "I just can. You do have a faculty for ferreting out unanswerable questions, don't you? Now let me ask you one. What is that long thing in your hand?"

"This? Why, it's a gun," said Huck a little self-consciously. He wished now that he hadn't brought it along.

"What is a gun?" asked George eagerly. He came closer and bent his head to sniff at the barrel.

"It's . . . to shoot things with."

"What is shoot?"

Huck looked around desperately. He couldn't bring himself to confess his former plan to this friendly, inquisitive denizen of another age.

"Do you know what an enemy is?" he asked tentatively.

"Of course. The meat-eating dinosaurs were my enemies," said George promptly. "They would have liked nothing better than to dine on me, the cannibals! That's why I have armor on my back and spikes on my tail. To protect myself."

"But I don't have armor or spikes," Huck told him quickly. "The gun is to protect me from my enemies. Shooting is what I do with it."

"You poor little mammal," murmured George pityingly. "That little stick would have done you little good had Allosaurus come leaping on you. But if it makes you feel safer, it probably serves its purpose. Tell me, do you think that by now we have observed enough of the social amenities? The odor of that banana is almost driving me crazy. My instinct is to eat it this minute."

"Please do," said Huck hastily. He watched while

the stegosaurus ambled over to the deep rut where the banana had fallen, pushed it out with his nose, and gobbled it down in a single bite.

"What do you eat when you don't have bananas?" he asked curiously.

"I eat what there is," George told him simply. "Here there is only sagebrush. It is tasty, once one gets used to it."

Huck stared at the stegosaurus in disbelief. He couldn't imagine anyone eating sagebrush, and yet there was no reason for the creature to lie about it.

"Someone's been digging up clumps of sage around our house," he remembered. "It's always at night."

"The proper time for serious feeding," agreed George. "Many mammals sleep when the sun goes down, and things are calmer then. Calmness aids digestion, so I find it is pleasanter to dine at night."

Huck's heart gave a happy thump. He had misjudged his grandfather after all. Opalo hadn't been responsible for that senseless business of clearing sage; George had been eating it. But that still didn't explain the holes about the hot spring.

"Somebody's been digging around here lately," Huck observed cautiously. "I suppose you watch while he does it. Have you ever talked to him?"

"No one's been digging here at all," denied George cheerfully. "I sharpen my tail in the ground now and then. It calms my nerves, although it does leave things a little messy."

Huck leaned up against a boulder and began to laugh. He couldn't remember when he had felt so lighthearted and pleased with the world. Bob and Nappy were wrong.

There was nothing at all the matter with his grandfather.

George came and stood beside him, his tiny dark eyes regarding him curiously.

"You are happy?"

"I'm so happy I could bust," Huck told him. "You don't know how glad I am that I found out about you. Now I know everything's going to be all right."

"You mustn't expect too much of me," declared the stegosaurus hastily. "Of course, I hold friendship in high esteem, and I shall do the best I can for you, but you really shouldn't count on me at all. Remember that my brain is not much larger than yours."

CHAPTER *FIVE*

HUCK WAS UNABLE
to visit with his new friend for several days, for on
the following morning Opalo declared that it was time
to make an expedition to the mountains for winter
firewood.

"Do we have to go?" Huck demanded in dismay.
It was the first time in his life that he had ever questioned his grandfather's decision, and Opalo looked at
him sharply.

"Do you wish me to freeze to death when winter
comes? Are you beginning to think, like the others, that
a medicine man has outlived his usefulness?"

"Oh, Grandfather, no!"

Huck hadn't meant to hurt his grandfather's feelings.
It was only that he had planned to go to the agency
today and ask Lily Franchere if she had a book on
dinosaurs he could borrow. Lily was very smart. She
had read many books and was planning to go on to
college, where she would read even more. Although
Huck didn't like to argue about it, George's sympathetic
allusions to Huck's small brain were very disturbing. If
he just knew enough about dinosaurs so that he could
discuss them intelligently, the stegosaurus might realize
that he had underestimated the boy's mind.

"It is long past the time when we start to bring in firewood," Opalo reminded him. "By this time last sum-

mer we had three wagonloads stacked in the shed. Now we have not even one. It is a long way to the mountains, and we have no squaws to do the work for us."

"I'll hitch up the wagon," offered Huck quickly. "We'd better get started. It will take Paint all day to get there."

As they rattled and bumped past the rocks which concealed the hot spring, Huck wondered if the stegosaurus was standing, camouflaged against the cliffs, watching them go by. They had spent such a delightful day together yesterday. George had been most interested in Huck's laundry, although a little critical. Even with a brain the size of a nut, he knew that it would serve no purpose at all, since everything would only get dirty all over again. Together they had peered down at the swimming pool in the summer resort and at the tiny figures splashing in the water. George couldn't understand that, either—not after Huck denied that the bathers were diving for food. George was sure that Huck was mistaken.

The boy wished he could stop long enough to say good-bye, to tell the stegosaurus that he would return in three days, but he knew that he couldn't. If he saw the dinosaur, Opalo would think he was having a vision, and the gigantic reptile would be sure to frighten old Paint. As a matter of fact, Huck was pretty sure that the strange behavior of the cayuse two days ago had been occasioned by a glimpse of the stegosaurus eating sagebrush by moonlight.

By early evening, however, Huck almost forgot about his new friend. As soon as they reached the mountains, Opalo made a hurried camp and set his grandson to work cutting wood. Once the old man had been strong enough to fell large trees with his ax, but now he had to content himself with cutting small saplings and hacking fallen limbs into lengths which could be piled into the wagon bed. Huck tried his best, but he, too, was only able to fell small trees. Although his muscles were developing, he was only eleven and it would take a few years before he could duplicate the work of a man. It was tiring work. His hands developed blisters, and his back ached before he had been at it an hour.

"Whose trees are these, Grandfather?" he asked once, straightening up to his full height to rest his muscles.

"They are our trees. The Great Spirit gave them to us."

"I know. But whose land are they on?"

"Our land," snapped Opalo. "Get back to work, Weewino."

Huck resumed work a little troubled. This was reservation land, of course, but he thought that probably they should have secured permission from the Council before helping themselves.

When it grew too dark to see, they ate cold food, then wrapped themselves in blankets and slept on the ground. At daybreak, work began again and continued all day long, and by evening the wagon bed was piled high with pitchy lengths of freshly cut fir.

"We will start home at daybreak," decided Opalo. "And go by the agency store. It is only a little out of our way. We will buy more of the yellow fruit from the land without snow. We have earned a treat."

Perhaps Paint knew that he was on his way home and that a good rest and supper awaited him, for, despite the heavy load, he made fair time the next day. It was midafternoon when Huck guided the wagon into the store lot.

He did not recognize the parked car next to them, or the driver, a woman who had remained behind the wheel. She had very red cheeks, brown curly hair, and blue eyes which twinkled behind shiny glasses. As Huck wrapped the reins around the whip handle, he was conscious that she was staring at him, and as he climbed down from the seat, she caught his eye.

"Hello," she said heartily.

"Hello," he answered, and ducked his head. He wasn't used to being greeted by strange ladies.

Opalo did not turn his head to look at the car or driver. He waited silently in the wagon while his grandson went inside after the bananas. He had spoken very little on the way home, and Huck realized he was very tired. Cutting wood was too hard for the old man. Perhaps Chief Whitewater was right; Grandfather might be better off close to town with someone to look after him.

Lily was waiting on customers when Huck entered the store, and until they turned around to see who had come in, he did not recognize them. Then he did. Although it was the first time he had seen them close at hand, he knew they were the twins who swam in the resort pool.

They were probably a year older than he, and they had round, freckled faces; round blue eyes; and red hair. The girl's was braided in two short pigtails; the boy wore his cut so short that it stood up in a stubble all over his head. Both wore blue jeans and blue-and-white checkered shirts. They recognized him, too, for

53

immediately they began to smile, wide smiles which stretched their mouths halfway across their faces.

"Hi," said the boy.

"Hi," echoed his sister, and Huck realized with surprise that even their voices were alike.

"Oh, do you know each other?" Lily smiled from behind the counter.

"We don't know his name," explained the girl. "Sometimes we see him on the cliff over the pool. We tried to get him to come down and go swimming, but he wouldn't."

"Well, then," declared Lily, "you ought to meet. This is Huck. He's a good friend of mine. And these are Joey and Joan Brown, Huck. They're spending the summer with their aunt, Mrs. Casey, who runs the summer resort just outside the reservation."

"She's not really our aunt," said Joey technically. "She's the professor's sister. And our mother and the professor got married, and they went back east so he could teach summer school at a college. And we didn't want to go, so we got to stay here till they get back."

"But she's as nice as a real aunt," put in Joan loyally. "Nicer than lots of them. Why didn't you come down to the pool when we asked you to? Auntie Casey wouldn't have minded. Were you afraid of the cliff? It is awfully steep."

"Of course he's not," Joey told her indignantly. "He's an Indian, and they aren't afraid of anything. I wish I were an Indian. At least part. We were hoping, when we came to stay with Auntie Casey, that we could get acquainted with some. But you're the first one we've met."

"Don't forget me," reminded Lily. "I'm an Indian."

"But you're a lady," Joey told her politely. "And you work in a store. That's different."

"So I do." Lily tried to smother her smile. She rang up their purchases on the cash register. "That will be a dollar and sixty-nine cents, please."

Joan turned to hand her a bill, then waited courteously while Lily made change.

"Could you come tomorrow?" Joey asked Huck. "It's a swell pool. During the week hardly anybody uses it but us. Not many people stay at the resort overnight, and those who do don't seem to have kids. Except little ones. Mostly people just drive down from the city on Saturday and Sunday to picnic and swim."

"Well, I don't know," said Huck weakly. They had been talking so fast, flinging remarks back and forth and answering each other's questions with such speed, that he had hardly had time to think. All he knew was that they had been wanting to meet him; that Joey, at least, admired Indians; and that they wanted him to come and swim with them in their pool. He could hardly believe it. It was the first time in his life that anyone had deliberately sought his company, and it made him a little dizzy.

"Then come the next day," urged Joan. At the sound of a horn, tooting from the parking lot, she tugged at her brother's arm. "Come on, Joey. Auntie Casey wants us to hurry."

"Just a minute." Joey brushed off her hand impatiently. He continued to stand where he was, waiting for Huck to make his purchases.

"What was it you wanted, Huck?" asked Lily gently.

"Bananas," said Huck, wishing that the twins would leave. He was flattered that they wanted to be friends, delighted at their invitation to go swimming, but the whole thing had happened so fast that he needed a moment to recover.

"We haven't one left," Lily told him regretfully. "And I don't think we'll get any more until it's cooler. They spoil so fast in the heat that we had to throw the last of them out."

"Oh." Huck's face fell. Grandfather would be disappointed. So would George, for Huck had already made up his mind to take his own share of bananas to the stegosaurus.

"Something else?" prompted Lily.

There was another reason why Huck had wanted to come to the store, but now he was embarrassed to ask. He took a deep breath and a quick look at the twins, who, despite a second summons from the horn outside, were still standing there beaming at him. Obviously they had no intention of leaving before he did, and it might be a long time before he got here again.

"Lily, do you have a book that tells about . . . dinosaurs?" he asked bravely.

"Why, no, Huck," she was beginning in a surprised tone, when Joan interrupted.

"Did you say dinosaurs? We've got a book about dinosaurs. Joey and I do. It's got pictures and everything. The professor gave it to us. It's at the cabin."

"How come you want to know about dinosaurs?" There was just a hint of suspicion in Joey's voice.

"I just heard about them," Huck told him. "They sound pretty interesting."

"You can look at our book when you come over to swim," promised Joan. "Joey, we've got to go. Auntie Casey is having a fit."

Obviously against his will, Joey allowed himself to be pulled out the door.

"Don't forget to come over," he called. "Come as soon as you can."

Huck waited inside until he heard the car drive out of the parking lot; then he, too, went out into the hot sunshine. As he let the screen door close behind him, he could hear voices coming around the side of the building, high-pitched, alarmingly familiar. He began to hurry as fast as he could.

The wagon, with its bed piled full of wood, was just as he had left it, and his grandfather was still sitting on the high seat staring straight ahead. But on the graveled parking lot beside the wagon stood the two persons whom Huck disliked most in all the world, Bob Catchum and Nappy Post.

"Aw, come on, Old Trout," Nappy was saying. "Tell us where you snitched all them sticks and what you're going to do with them."

"Maybe he's going to make heap big medicine," suggested Bob. "Is that what you're going to do, Old Trout?"

If Opalo heard them, he gave no sign. His wide-brimmed hat shaded eyes which did not move from the painted side of the building.

"Bet he's going to make a big fire and scare off evil spirits," declared Nappy. "How about letting us see one of them evil spirits right now, Old Trout? I'd sure like to see one."

Huck's racing feet carried him to where the boys were standing, and he struck out blindly with both fists. He'd known that this would happen eventually. He meant to hit them and hit them until they begged for mercy. He'd teach them to say such things to his grandfather.

They had not heard him coming, and Nappy, taken unaware, was knocked to the ground. Bob, however, whirled around and began fighting back. He was a little taller than Huck, and huskier besides, and his fist smashed into Huck's face with a force which made him stagger.

"Stop that," ordered Opalo angrily from the wagon, and his voice had suddenly shed its years and snapped with authority. Although he spoke in Klickitat, there was no mistaking the command, and the battle ceased abruptly.

Bob's arm fell to his side, and the clenched fist straightened slowly. Nappy, who had scrambled to his feet and was preparing to join in, stayed where he was. Huck looked up and was startled by what he saw. Grandfather looked like a stranger. His eyes were blazing; his lips were drawn back from his yellow teeth. He looked—scary.

"Get into the wagon, Weewino," he ordered, and as Huck obeyed, his contemptuous, angry eyes inspected the two boys on the ground. "Go home and tell your parents they have insolent jackals for sons."

"What did he say to us, Huck?" asked Bob. His voice sounded a little uneasy.

"He said you'd better watch your step," called Huck, gathering up the reins. He was very proud of Grandfather. He'd certainly shown those two what was what. They'd think twice before they made fun of him again. "He said if you step out of line once more, he'll really put an evil spell on you."

The moment he said it, he knew he'd gone too far. If he'd only left things as they were, Bob and Nappy would have remained chastised. But promising evil spells was too much. They both began to laugh.

"Going to make big medicine, huh?" taunted Nappy. "Maybe call up a monster to eat us up?"

"If he doesn't, I will," promised Huck, pulling on the lines as a signal for Paint to back up. He spoke confidently, for the word "monster" had given him the most brilliant idea of his life. He'd ask his friend George to frighten these two enemies. The stegosaurus would be happy to help. All he'd have to do would be to show himself briefly, and they'd never stop running.

"Oh, yeah?" Bob laughed.

"How about tomorrow?" asked Huck.

"Tomorrow?" They exchanged surprised glances.

"Why, he's as wacky as his old man," observed Bob in astonishment.

"You'll see," shrieked Huck angrily. "You meet me at the hot spring on our land, and I'll show you. About noon. You'll see whether I'm wacky or not. Unless you're too chicken to show up."

"We'll be there," promised Nappy.

CHAPTER *SIX*

during the next morning, Huck was afraid he would
not be able to keep his appointment with Nappy and
Bob. His grandfather set him to unloading firewood
from the wagon as soon as they finished their breakfast.

"Tomorrow we must return to the mountains for another load," he announced firmly. "It will take much
wood to see me through the winter."

At the beginning, Opalo had tried to help with the
work, but he moved painfully and with an obvious ef-
fort. He was still tired from the long trip and the
strenuous exercise of cutting and gathering sticks. Finally he had to admit that it was too much for him
and went back into the house.

Huck worked on alone. He threw the pitchy sticks to
the ground as fast as he could, not stopping to stack and
pile. That would be done later when he had more time.
He kept an anxious eye on the sun, watching it climb
higher and higher in the sky. He had set noon as the
hour for Nappy and Bob to meet him at the hot
spring, feeling sure that it would give him plenty of
time to arrive first and arrange matters with the stegosaurus. He had completely forgotten about unloading
the firewood.

But Opalo had not forgotten. Nor would he hear of

postponing the task. Perhaps, Huck thought, as the straggly mound of sticks on the ground began to spread out and grow higher under his efforts, Grandfather was doing this on purpose. Perhaps it was his way of keeping his grandson out of another fight.

Opalo must have heard the challenge Huck had thrown over his shoulder as he drove out of the parking lot yesterday, but he had not mentioned it then or later. He had only said that the wagon must be emptied of wood before Huck could leave the premises. Now Huck wondered what his grandfather had thought of his promise to produce a monster for Nappy and Bob. That hadn't been mentioned either.

When the last fragment of bark bounced onto the heap and all that remained on the wagon bed were scattered bits of moss, Huck jumped down and ran into the house. His grandfather was sound asleep, his gray braids spread over the blanket which covered the straw-filled tick, his slightly open mouth giving off gentle, regular snores. Huck tiptoed outside without awakening him. Grandfather needed to sleep, and, besides, he might say that the wood must now be stacked before his grandson was free to leave.

With an upward glance at the sun, which was fast approaching noon, he started down the road at a loping trot. He wanted to get there—he must get there—before Nappy and Bob, so that he could coach George in the role he was expected to play. Of course, there wasn't very much for the stegosaurus to do—just step forward so he could be seen and flourish his tail a little. He wouldn't have to say a word. As soon as they had recovered from their initial fright, Bob and Nappy would take to their heels. But the story of what they had witnessed would get around. After this, people would have nothing but respect for Huck and his grandfather. They'd be afraid to have anything else.

As he came in sight of the rocky spur concealing the hot spring, Huck increased his gait to a run. Approaching from the opposite direction were two unmistakable figures, one on each side of the road. Nappy and Bob were riding their bicycles to the meeting place, and in order to avoid the ruts cut by wagon wheels, they were staying close to the edges. Even so, the rough ground made pedaling difficult. If he hurried, he could reach the spring before they did.

Bob and Nappy had seen him by this time. They shouted something as he reached the rocks, but they were too far away for Huck to understand what they said. As he dashed around the encircling spur, he was panting so hard he could hardly call out.

"George! Where are you?"

The rocky cliff before him began to waver back and forth, and the next moment the irregular shape of the stegosaurus became visible.

"My little friend! Have you brought me a banana?"

"No. I want you to do something for me. Help me." There was little time for explanation and, breathless as he was, Huck hoped that he could make his brief instructions clear. "Two boys are coming here. Bad boys. Enemies. You hide. I'll say some words. Wave my arms. When I call your name, come out. Let them see you."

"Perhaps they're just passing by!" The great tail,

which had been wagging in a friendly fashion, halted in midair.

"I'll bring them. Now," promised Huck. "You hide till I call you."

Without waiting to make sure he was understood, he turned and dashed back around the rocks. He was just in time. Nappy and Bob had given up pedaling. They were walking, wheeling their bicycles beside them.

"Well, where is it?" shouted Bob. "Where's the monster?"

"You'll see," Huck told him darkly. He hoped that he had said enough to make George understand what was expected of him.

"You don't look much like a medicine man to me," criticized Nappy, leaning his bike up against the boulder. "You could at least have put some paint on your face and a feather in your hair."

"Why didn't you borrow some of Old Trout's stuff, Huckleberry?" agreed Bob quickly. "How do you expect to call up a monster looking like you always do?"

"The monster is my friend," announced Huck grandly. "He will come when I call. And when he does, you two had better get out of here fast. That's all I can say."

"Sure, sure." Nappy laughed. "Only show him to us first."

"Come on," said Huck angrily. He led the way around the rocks, with Nappy and Bob following close on his heels.

At noon the sun fell full into the area surrounding the spring, dissolving the shadows on the tall cliff of sedimentary rock so that it looked uniformly brownish gray.

Remembering the markings of orange and yellow and purple which mottled the hard skin of the stegosaurus, Huck inspected the side of the cliff anxiously. He was relieved that the reptile had obeyed his instructions and had secreted himself in a way which made him completely invisible. It would be too bad to spoil the effect before he was ready.

"Come on," prompted Bob.

"Where's your monster?" demanded Nappy.

"You'll see," promised Huck. He walked over and stood beside the spring, motioning the two boys to stay where they were beside the rocky spur. "I'll call him now. You just keep your eyes open."

Giggling and poking each other, Nappy and Bob leaned against the boulder, their delighted eyes daring him to do his worst.

Huck had never seen his grandfather call a spirit. Although Opalo made frequent references to the time when he had served his tribe as a medicine man, he no longer practiced his profession, and Huck had never asked for details. He was not sure what was expected of him, but, then, neither Bob nor Nappy would know the old form. He lifted his right hand and focused his black eyes on the cloudless sky which arced overhead. For the first time in his life, he was grateful that he knew Klickitat. It had always been a little embarrassing before to be the only one in the school who could speak a tribal tongue so efficiently, but the knowledge had come in useful after all.

"Baa, baa, black sheep," he began solemnly, and the words in translation bore no resemblance to their English original. "Have you any wool? Yes, sir. Yes, sir.

Three bags full. One for my master. One for my dame. One for the little boy who lives in the lane."

Years ago, when he was very small and before his mother died, she had taught him that poem. He had almost forgotten about it, but now the words came back to him when he needed them.

At the end he paused significantly, trying to stare down the two by the boulder as Opalo had done yesterday. They had stopped giggling, and although he had to admit that they looked more expectant than frightened, they were giving him their full attention. It was the proper moment, and he broke into English.

"George! Come on out, George!"

He pointed commandingly at the cliff, waiting for the rough gray stones to move and re-sort themselves into the jagged form of a stegosaurus. Nothing happened, so he called again more sharply.

"George! Don't you hear me? George! Now!"

Bob and Nappy began to laugh, and the sound was magnified and prolonged in an echo which bounced back and forth between the cliff and the rocky spur. Still no ponderous shape stepped out from the rocks.

Huck continued to call. He couldn't think what had happened. Even if Huck had not made himself clear, the stegosaurus ought to answer to his name. That didn't take any brains. All he had to do was step forward from the spot where he was standing.

"Where's your monster, Huckleberry?" Nappy stopped laughing long enough to shout the question. "What happened to your hocus-pocus mumbo jumbo? Something go wrong?"

Huck ran over to the cliff and began feeling along the

66

rocks with his hands. If he could just touch hard skin or one of those bony shields with his fingers, he might be able to pull the reptile forward so that it would be visible. At the same time he kept calling out, trying to explain things so that George would understand and co-operate.

"George, please! They don't believe you're here. Show them, George. They're enemies. They're mean and bad."

"Shut up!" The echo made Bob's voice sound as though it was coming from three sides. He spoke sharply, and until Nappy stopped laughing and demanded. "What for?" Huck thought Bob had been speaking to him.

"Because he's really wacky," said Bob uneasily. "Anybody is who thinks he can call up monsters. And he does. Can't you see he actually believes it? He's as bad as his old man."

"So what?" asked Nappy.

"So we better get out of here," declared Bob. "People that are really wacky are liable to do anything. Besides, they make me feel funny. I don't like to be around them."

Nappy must have agreed, because when Huck turned around, they were both gone.

There was no use feeling along the cliff any longer, so he stopped. So far as he was concerned, he never wanted to see the stegosaurus again. George was nothing but an ugly, stupid monster who should have died millions of years ago—provided, of course, that he really was a stegosaurus. Huck had only the creature's word for that, and what did the word of anyone so undependable and selfish really mean? George must have heard Nappy and Bob laughing. Even though he possessed a very small brain, he must have known that they were making fun of Huck. And George had insisted that he was Huck's friend. That was a lie. Friends didn't stand silently by when they knew they were needed.

To his dismay, a drop of water ran down Huck's cheek and splashed on the rocky ground. Why, he was crying. It was something he hadn't done since his mother died. He could hardly remember the last time he had cried. Opalo had taught him that tears were unmanly, and Huck had always been able to hold them back. But here he was, crying like a baby, and the ugly stegosaurus, the cause of the tears, was undoubtedly crouched invisibly against the cliff, enjoying the spectacle.

Huck knew that he must get out of there, but he couldn't go home, not just yet, for then he would have to return to the road, and Nappy and Bob might be lingering about on the other side of the rocks. It left only one place to go, the cliff overlooking the summer resort. He trotted off as fast as he could go, fearful that another tear might betray him.

Only the twins were occupying the pool, and they did not see him, for Huck threw himself face down on the ground and wriggled to the edge so that only the top of his head would be visible. The water had never looked so inviting. It was bluer than the sky, bluer than the Warm Springs River or Olallie Lake in the mountains, where they had cut the firewood.

There was a diving board at one end of the pool, and as Huck watched, Joey climbed up and jumped back into the water with a great splash. It was not a very good dive, because he lifted his head at the last minute. If Huck had only been there, he could have told Joey what he was doing wrong. A minute later, Joan climbed out of the water and ran around to the board to dive in exactly as her brother had done. It was a real belly flop, and it made Huck wince to watch. Belly flops hurt. Someone ought to show them what they were doing wrong.

He stood up and walked over to the beginning of the old trail which zigzagged crookedly down the side of the cliff. It was his duty, plain enough, to point out their mistakes to the twins. Besides, he had been invited.

They saw him coming before he was halfway down, for the trail was old and clogged with loose pebbles and dirt. Huck had to pick his way carefully, pushing debris away with his foot and clinging to larger rocks until it had scattered down the side. It gave him a pleasant sense of being wanted to hear their welcoming whoops as they climbed out of the water and rushed over to the wire fence at the bottom of the cliff.

"Hurry up," yelled Joey enthusiastically.

"No, don't!" warned Joan. "Take your time. Be careful you don't fall."

Apparently that started some small controversy between them, for he could see them talking earnestly to each other. They were too far away to catch what they were saying, but they did not call to him after that. They merely stood waiting by the fence, which marked the dividing line between the reservation and land belonging to the resort, and he could see that they were both smiling broadly. He was glad of those smiles, thankful that someone wanted to be friends with him.

"That's an awful scary trail," said Joan respectfully as Huck finally slid to the bottom, along with a last shower of pebbles. "At least it looks like it is."

"It's nothing for him," Joey insisted promptly. "We're sure glad you could come today, Huck."

"Auntie Casey will be, too," confided Joan as he climbed over the fence. "We told her all about meeting you in the store yesterday."

"Did you bring your swimming trunks?" asked Joey. And when Huck shook his head blankly, he added, "Oh, that's all right. There's some here. People keep forgetting them. Sometimes they never bother to come back after them at all, so after a while Auntie Casey just puts them all in a big box. We can probably find a pair to fit you."

Chattering gaily, one on each side, they escorted Huck over the rough ground and onto the wide gray strip surrounding the pool. It was paving, Huck discovered. From the top of the cliff he had never been able to decide whether it was cement or sand.

"Come with me," urged Joey. "The suits are in the bathhouse."

Luckily, there was a pair of bathing trunks which fit Huck exactly, and he put them on feeling very elegant and well dressed. He had never worn such a thing before, which was one reason why he had stopped

71

swimming with the boys at school. When he was small, it hadn't mattered. Lots of little kids swam in under-clothes or worn-out jeans, but by the time they were ten or eleven, their families had purchased proper bath-ing trunks for them. Huck hadn't wanted to ask his grandfather to spend the money for such a luxury. He wasn't at all sure that Opalo had that much money.

"Come on," urged Joey impatiently. "Let's go."

The water in the pool felt wonderful. There was a shallow end and a deep one, and the diving board had a bouncy spring which no makeshift plank over a river could possibly duplicate. Huck showed the twins what they were doing wrong in their dives, and they im-mediately set about correcting their mistakes.

"We didn't swim too much before we came here," confessed Joey. "We live on a ranch about seventy miles away, and there's not much water. None for swim-ming."

"And before that we lived in a town where there was a pool, but it was always so crowded you could hardly swim," continued Joan. "Besides, we didn't get to go there much. Our own father died and mother had to work, and the lady who took care of us wouldn't take us there."

"But you can sure swim good," said Joey. "Better than anybody I ever saw."

"Lots of people swim better than I do," Huck ad-mitted, but it gave him a warm, comforting feeling to be admired.

The brown-haired lady who had spoken to Huck yesterday from the car in the parking lot came around the corner of the house carrying a tray.

72

"How about some lemonade and cookies?" she called.

Joey and Joan began climbing out of the pool immediately, and Huck followed a little more slowly. He wasn't sure the invitation included him, even though he could count three glasses on the tray.

"This is our friend Huck, Auntie Casey," introduced Joey proudly.

"Hello, Huck." Blues eyes twinkled at him from behind the shiny glasses. "I saw you yesterday at the agency with your grandfather."

"Yes, ma'am," he said shyly, wondering how she could know that Opalo was his grandfather.

"I have an Indian woman working for me," she explained, as though she read his thoughts. "Mildred Post. She told me about you."

Mildred Post was Nappy's aunt. Huck ducked his head, wondering exactly what Mildred had told Mrs. Casey.

They sat in canvas chairs alongside the pool while they drank their lemonade and ate the frosted cookies. At first Huck was afraid that Mrs. Casey meant to stay and talk to them. She kept smiling at him, as the twins had done, asking him questions about how old he was and what grade he was in at school. But when he only answered in polite monosyllables, she went back to the house. Huck was relieved to see her go. If she had discussed him with Mildred Post, she probably knew all those things anyway. Even worse, she had probably heard the gossip about his grandfather. He hoped she hadn't told the twins.

"Do you want to look at the book about dinosaurs now?" asked Joan, licking a bit of frosting from her fingers. "I went in and got it while you and Joey were in the bathhouse."

They both looked at him expectantly, awaiting his answer, so Huck nodded. He really didn't want to see the book. In the last hour he had almost forgotten the humiliating experience at the hot spring, but now it all came back to him. He remembered Nappy and Bob standing beside the boulder, laughing, and his own frantic pleas to George to show himself. No wonder the two had decided there was something mentally wrong with him. He must have looked really crazy shouting to an invisible monster which wouldn't materialize.

"It's over here." Joan smiled happily at his reluctant nod. "I'll get it."

"We know quite a lot about dinosaurs," confided Joey. "The professor, our new father, is an archaeologist, and he told us. But we know some other things, too, that we found out by ourselves."

Joan returned with a large gray book, which she put on Huck's lap. Then she squatted down beside him so she could turn the pages. Joey pulled his chair close on the other side.

"Here's where they start," Joan told him. "Dinosaurs began in the Triassic age, and that was 220,000,000 years ago."

"Skip over to where it's interesting," ordered Joey.

Joan seemed to know exactly what he meant. Pages of text and illustrations flipped by as she turned them.

"This is the upper Jurassic period," she announced, stopping at the illustration of a ponderous reptile with a long, giraffelike neck and a trailing, lizardlike tail.

"This is Brontosaurus, the Thunder Lizard. They called him that because he was so big that they think the ground rumbled when he walked."

Huck inspected the drawing carefully. If this was a dinosaur, perhaps George was wrong in claiming kinship. This reptile had no armored shields along its back, no spikes on its tail, and its head was lifted high instead of drooping low.

"And this is Allosaurus." Joan turned the page, pausing for Huck to examine the dinosaur pictured there. "He ate meat, especially Brontosauruses. I guess he was pretty terrible."

This picture didn't resemble George either. The reptile walked on two hind legs, for the front limbs were short and hung down like hands, ending in great hooked talons instead of huge padded feet.

Again Joan turned the page, waiting while Huck's startled eyes took in the next illustration. There was the humped-up, irregular form; the small, low-hung head; the rows of upright, bony plates along the back; and the long tail with its four ferocious spikes.

"It's him!" he whispered involuntarily. "It's George!"

Joey jumped to his feet and began hopping up and down.

"Did you hear that, Joan? He knows him! He knows George! Oh, I just knew he was here. As soon as I heard about all the mineral springs, I had a feeling we'd find him here!"

Joan's blue eyes were shining, and she stood up so quickly that the book tumbled to the pavement.

"Where is he?" she cried happily. "You've got to take us to him, Huck. George is a friend of ours."

CHAPTER *SEVEN*

HUCK COULD HARDLY BELIEVE his own ears. For a few minutes he forgot that George had betrayed him and made him look ridiculous. Here, at last, was someone who would back up his story, who would realize that he was telling the truth about the gigantic creature who could come and go so silently among the rimrock.

There was no doubt that the twins were acquainted with George. They knew him even better than Huck did.

Once, they told him eagerly, the stegosaurus had made his home among the sedimentary cliffs of their own ranch on Cricket Creek. He had been their friend. Why, it was they who had given him the name of George, because it had been so many years since anyone had called him by his original name that he had completely forgotten what it was. He had played a part in capturing a bank robber and had helped them discover the fossilized bone of Eohippus, the tiny three-toed horse.

George had been forced to take leave of his friends when he had unthinkingly closed up the single mineral spring on Cricket Creek. Since it supplied his drinking water, they knew that wherever he settled it would have to be close to a similar spring.

"We've been to every hot spring that we could find,"

Joey told him. "But there's so many around here, and lots of them are too far away to walk to. Of course, we couldn't tell Auntie Casey why we wanted to go to the other springs, or she might have driven us in the car."

"And just think," sighed Joan. "The right spring, the one George had picked, was only a little way from where we've been living."

"Why couldn't you tell your aunt?" Huck wondered. "Wouldn't she have believed you?"

"Nobody does," said Joey gravely. "George is a secret that you have to keep to yourself. If you don't, people think you're imagining things or that you've had a sunstroke."

"But if they saw him themselves? If you took someone there so they could see that you weren't making it up——"

"Oh, you mustn't ever do that," objected Joan quickly. "George is very shy! That might scare him away for good. He's afraid of people. So far as we know, you're the only one who has ever laid eyes on him for millions of years. Besides us, of course."

For the first time, Huck began to see his mistake.

"Oh," he said weakly. "That's why he wouldn't come out when I called him to scare Nappy and Bob."

"What do you mean?" demanded Joey sharply.

Unhappily, Huck told them that story. He didn't confess that it was because Nappy and Bob had been teasing his grandfather, or why. He preferred to have the twins think that his was the usual Indian family on the reservation and that in his youth Opalo had worked in lumber or at farming instead of serving as a medicine man. But he did admit that he and Nappy and Bob were not on friendly terms, that they had battled more than once, and that he had thought it would serve them right to be scared.

"That was a terrible thing to do to George," said Joey severely when Huck had finished. "He wouldn't understand at all. He'll think you mean to bring all kinds of people there to stare at him, and he'll be awfully upset. He'll go away again."

"Maybe he won't leave till after dark," Joan suggested hopefully. "He stays close to the cliffs in the daytime."

"We'd better go there right away," decided Joey, standing up. "If we can just catch him before he leaves, and explain things, maybe he won't go away."

Once again Huck wished he had never met the stegosaurus. The ways things looked now, George might cost him the friendship of the twins. Clearly the dinosaur came first in their affections, while he himself was just a newcomer. If he had frightened George away, Joey and Joan would never forgive him, and it wasn't his fault at all. George had told Huck many things that afternoon they had spent washing and drying clothes, but he hadn't once said not to bring anyone else to the hot spring.

Auntie Casey said the twins might walk partway home with Huck, and they crossed the cleared space beyond the pool and climbed over the wire fence.

"It's a long way up there," shivered Joan, looking up at the trail. "Why don't we go back and around by the road?"

"It takes too long," said Joey briefly.

"I'll go ahead," offered Huck. "You watch where I put my feet, Joan, and put yours there, too. And don't look back down."

The cliff was high and almost straight up and down. It took them some time to reach the top by means of the straggling trail, but eventually they made it.

"So this is what's up here," observed Joey in an interested tone as he stared around. "I've always meant to climb up sometime and see, but I never got around to it."

They were standing on a plateau, and before them stretched the flat, barren acres which comprised the upper portion of the reservation. The ground was not so even as it had appeared from below and was dotted with stunted juniper and sage. To their left, the cliff continued upward for another fifty feet or more, forming the third side of the enclosure which sheltered the spring. The road, connecting Opalo's acres to the agency, was straight ahead but concealed from view by vigorous stands of dusty sagebrush.

"Where is it?" demanded Joan anxiously. "Where's the hot spring? We ought to get there as quick as we can."

Silently, Huck motioned them to follow as he led the way through the narrow gap formed by the side of the cliff and the spur of rock which ran around from the front. He hoped desperately that the stegosaurus was still there and would answer their call, but, without a ripe banana for bait, he couldn't have much faith.

"He's been here!" cried Joey in excitement as they entered the enclosure. "Look at those holes, Joan. He's been sharpening his tail."

"And the spring's the way he likes it, too." Joan hurried over to bend down and touch a tentative finger in the water. She straightened up and said, "Ouch!" But she was smiling all the while.

"George!" shouted Joey. "George, can you hear me? It's us. It's your friends, Joey and Joan. Remember?"

His voice echoed against the rocky walls, bouncing back and forth long after he had stopped.

Huck's eyes moved anxiously from side to side. The stegosaurus might be anywhere. Once he had been standing against the boulder at the entrance. That was the first time, the time he snatched the banana from Huck's hand. The second time he had evolved from the face of the cliff. It didn't matter where he stood. So long as it was against rock, he melted into the background and became invisible.

Joan added her entreaties to those of her twin.

"Please come out, George. This is Joan. You remember us, don't you? It was only last summer that you went away. You can't have forgotten so soon."

Still there was no answering voice, no jagged, cumbersome shape appearing like a silent rockslide. Huck's face grew long with worry. He had spent a wonderful afternoon, and the twins had talked as though it was to be the first of many like it. They might withdraw their friendship if George wouldn't show himself. If only he could let the stegosaurus know that he realized his own mistake.

"George," Huck called as soon as Joan stopped. "George, this is Huck. I want to tell you that I'm sorry about bringing those two boys here this morning. I didn't understand. It was a stupid thing to do, and I'm sorry. Please come out, George."

The echo died away, and when there was still no answer he tried again.

"I'll never do it again, George. I'll never tell another soul about you, and I'll never bring anyone here again. I'll protect you. I'll keep everyone away and not let them come close to you. I wouldn't have brought Joey and Joan, but they said they were your friends. They said they knew you already."

"Naturally they know me. At least you have brains enough to recognize that truth when you hear it!" The voice was sharp and seemed to come from the center of the rocky cliff. Then the cliff began to shift around, and a moment later the stegosaurus padded down the side on huge cushioned feet.

"Joey! Joan! My dear, dear friends," cried George joyfully. "I've been wondering when you would come. It's taken you such a long time."

"We didn't know where you'd gone," explained Joey. "You didn't tell us."

"I didn't have to. You have brains," chided George. "I knew you could find me, once you used your brains. You're not like this poor mammal here. His brain is even smaller than mine. That's why I must forgive him for bringing those other mammals here. He didn't know any better."

"Why didn't you come out when we first called you, George?" asked Joan, patting the rough head, which was bent even lower so she could reach it.

"That's what my instinct told me to do," confessed George. "But I have my pride, too. *He* had to apologize first. He did it very nicely, too, I thought. And you heard him promise to protect me? I was very touched. I want you both to help me look after him from now on."

"Look after Huck?" repeated Joey in surprise. "But, George, he's——"

"I know. A pitiful case," interrupted the stegosaurus. "That's why we must take care of him, you and I. So far as I can determine, he doesn't even have instinct to fall back on."

CHAPTER *EIGHT*

"I DON'T GET IT," confessed Joey. He and his sister had been swimming, perfecting the dives which Huck had taught them yesterday, and now they were stretched out in the sun beside the pool. "What do you suppose ever gave George the idea that Huck was dumb and needed to be looked after?"

"I don't know." Joan's dripping pigtails bounced with the motion of her head. "But you know how he is. He wouldn't even listen to us. Once George gets an idea, you can't ever change his mind."

"But Huck, of all people! Huck's an Indian, and they're smart. They don't have to have anybody to look after them. They can live in the woods, and kill game to eat, and make their own clothes out of skin, and all kinds of things that we can't do."

"I don't think they do those things anymore," his sister reminded him honestly. "That's only in books. Auntie Casey says the Indians on this reservation live just like anybody else. They buy their food and clothes in stores."

"But they don't have to. It's only because they want to. If you or I happened to be lost in the woods, we wouldn't know what to do. But you put an Indian in the same woods and he'd find his way home in

84

nothing flat. And he wouldn't starve on the way, either."

"You mean he could do all that just because he's an Indian?"

"Sure."

"Girl Indians, too?"

"Well . . ." Joey wasn't too sure about that, but since he had already made such a flat statement, he hated to back down. "Probably not so easy, but they'd know something about it."

Joan stood up, her wet bathing suit leaving a dark spot on the cement where she had been sitting.

"Then let's go ask Mildred what she'd do if she were lost in the woods."

"Now?" objected Joey quickly. "I thought you wanted to swim some more."

"Now," said Joan in a firm voice. "Before you forget what you just said. Mildred's cleaning the end cabin this morning. I saw her go there with the mop and scrub bucket."

There were four cabins for overnight guests, but they were seldom occupied. Most people preferred more luxurious accommodations than the resort could provide. Auntie Casey didn't mind. She said that her wants were few and that the revenue provided on Saturday and Sunday by visitors who drove the fast highways from the city to picnic in the shade of the cottonwoods and swim in the pool was quite enough for her needs. Nevertheless, the rustic cabins were kept in spotless condition, and it was Mildred's job to clean them once a week.

Joan ran ahead, with Joey following a little more

slowly. She called from the bottom step, for they had been cautioned more than once about tracking up wet floors, and after a minute Mildred came to stand in the doorway.

She was a plump woman in her middle forties, with short black hair, which needed trimming. She wore a green cotton housedress, a silver wristwatch with a dark band, and earrings with large red stones. She was carrying a string mop, which dripped a trail of rather gray water.

"Mildred," began Joan quickly, before Joey had a chance to hint at a solution. "Whàt would you do if you were lost in the woods?"

The smile faded from Mildred's cheerful brown face, and she looked worried.

"You mustn't go into the woods," she told them. "There's bears and wildcats, maybe cougars."

"We aren't going there." Now that the interview was under way, Joey intended to see that it went well. "We want to know how you'd find your way home if you got lost."

"I'm not going into the woods," declared Mildred fervently. "Not me. What do I want to go there for?"

"But suppose you did," insisted Joey. "Suppose you were there and you wanted to get home. You'd find a stream, wouldn't you? And see which way it was running? And look at the moss on the trees, to see which side was thickest?"

"That's not fair, Joey," his sister told him angrily. "You read that in a book, and you're telling her what to say."

"She knows what to say, all right. She just doesn't

understand what we mean," claimed Joey. "That's what you'd do, wouldn't you, Mildred? Tell direction by how the moss grows, and stuff like that?"

"You're kidding, Joey." Mildred laughed, putting down her wet mop and leaning against the doorjamb to enjoy the joke. "What do you think I am? A blanket Indian?"

"What's a blanket Indian?"

"One of the old-timers. You know, like you see on TV. They just stand around, wrapped in a blanket, and say 'How!'" Mildred laughed harder than ever. "The guys that dream that stuff up! Where do you suppose they get it anyhow?"

"See?" said Joan pointedly.

"Aren't there any old-timers—any blanket Indians anymore at all?" asked Joey plaintively.

Mildred must have sensed his disappointment, because she tried to stop laughing.

"Not very many. Of course, there's Martha Whitewater, the chief's grandmother. She's a real one for sure. The trouble she gives us at the Huckleberry Festival! And I suppose she'll have to go all through it again this year, all that stuff about rose hips and chokecherries. But we just put up with it and let her have her way. After all, she's the chief's grandmother. And it makes her feel better, poor old thing."

"Is she the only one?" asked Joan when Mildred, overcome by sudden pity, fell silent.

"There's Old Opalo," chuckled Mildred, recovering her good humor. "Now there's a real blanket Indian for you. But he's crazy as a bedbug. He used to be a medicine man, they tell me, back when people believed

87

in such stuff. I suppose that's what set him off: people stopped believing. I've never had much to do with him. I only see him at the festivals, when he shows up at the Longhouse in all his paint and feathers. He lives down here somewhere, all alone most of the time, except in summer when they let his great-grandson come out and stay with him. That's not so hot, either. It isn't right for a young boy to stay with a crazy old man. People are starting to talk."

"What's the boy's name?" demanded Joey quickly.

"Huck," answered Mildred promptly. "I guess it's short for Huckleberry. My nephew, Nappy, knows him, and that's what he calls him. Imagine saddling a kid with a name like Huckleberry!"

"Did you say Nappy?" asked Joan.

"It's short for Napoleon," said Mildred. "I don't care so much for that name, either, but at least it's real. There was a famous general named that. My sister-in-law has kind of highfalutin ideas sometimes. But, like I was saying, Nappy knows Huckleberry real well, and he says he gets a little queerer every year. The other kids all talk about it. I don't think the chief ought to let him spend his summers out here with his grandpa. It's not good."

Auntie Casey's voice came floating through the cottonwoods, which grew between the cabins and the main house.

"Joey! Joan! If you're driving into the agency with me, get out of the pool! I'm almost ready to leave."

Mildred picked up her mop hastily.

"I better get back to work. Your aunt doesn't like it

when she catches me standing talking. But a person can't be expected to work every minute."

The twins always enjoyed driving in to the agency, and they hurried to the house to change their clothes. Mildred's remarks about Huck and his grandfather were a little upsetting. Huck hadn't appeared odd to them. He had seemed like any other normal boy. But if Mildred was right, he shouldn't be living with someone who was mentally unbalanced. It might be dangerous.

Auntie Casey's car was not new, but it was sturdy, and it did not take long to cover the graveled road in to the agency store. The nearest town was thirty miles away, so the residents and visitors at the resort always went to the agency to buy groceries. Auntie Casey drove into the parking lot, and all three of them went inside.

Lily Franchere was behind the counter as usual, and two boys about the same age as the twins were standing beside the case filled with soda pop, trying to make up their minds about flavors. Joan nudged her brother to call his attention to the fact that they were Indians, but for some reason Joey seemed to have lost some of his earlier desire to meet members of that race. He accompanied his aunt and Joan to the counter without a second look at the boys.

"Hi, Lily," said Auntie Casey cordially. "The hot spell still's hanging on, isn't it?"

"It certainly is." Lily smiled. "But next winter we'll wish we had a little of it."

The two boys had finally made a selection and were

drinking the pop there so they wouldn't have to pay extra for the bottles. Lily called to them, and they came over to the counter.

"You were anxious to meet some of our people, Joey," she said. "This is Bob Catchum and Nappy Post. Mrs. Casey, Joan and Joey Brown."

The twins recognized the names instantly. These must be the two who were making all the trouble for Huck, the two enemies he had taken to the hot spring. They did not look very formidable as they stood there grinning in an embarrassed fashion. They looked like two ordinary twelve-year-old boys, with very tanned skin, wearing T-shirts and jeans. But, of course, you could never tell.

"Post," repeated Auntie Casey, beaming at the two boys. "Are you any relation to Mildred?"

"She's my aunt," admitted Nappy, and immediately took a long swig from his pop bottle.

Auntie Casey turned back to Lily and began giving her the grocery order.

"Don't forget bananas, Auntie Casey," Joan reminded her. Huck had told them how much George enjoyed bananas, and they wanted to take him one or two as a present.

"We haven't any bananas," apologized Lily. "The last bunch we had spoiled before we could get rid of it. I've had several customers who've asked for them lately, too."

"Huck wanted bananas the last time we were here," said Joey. He seemed to linger over the first word a little longer than he needed to.

"I remember." Lily smiled.

"We like Huck," announced Joey loudly. "He's a good guy."

Nappy and Bob exchanged quick glances of surprise, and Joan realized that Joey was deliberately lining himself up against Huck's enemies.

"Yes, he is," agreed Auntie Casey, beaming on everyone. "He came over yesterday and swam in the pool with the children. Such a polite youngster, but very shy."

"He is shy," said Lily. "I'm afraid he's very slow to make friends. He's always alone, poor little thing."

Bob choked on a swallow of pop and turned his back.

"Huckleberry's not shy," Nappy declared. "Not when you get to know him, he isn't."

"He's still a good guy," insisted Joey fiercely. "And he's a friend of ours, Napoleon."

A tinge of red crept into Nappy's brown face. He looked at Joey in surprise; then he, too, turned and carried his empty pop bottle back to the rack. Bob followed, and from the corner of her eye, Joan could see them whispering together all the time Auntie Casey was finishing her shopping. Both boys were looking the other way when they finally left the store.

"You know," said Joey in a low voice as they preceded Auntie Casey to the parking lot, "I guess George was partly right after all."

"What do you mean?" asked Joan.

"Well, Huck's not dumb," he told her thoughtfully. "But he does need somebody to help him."

CHAPTER *NINE*

THE NEXT DAY
was Saturday, and because weekends were busy times at the pool, the twins had no opportunity to return to the hot spring to visit with George.

Picnickers began arriving early in the morning. They put their lunch baskets on tables under the cottonwoods and immediately hurried to change into bathing suits. Joan and Joey helped wherever they were needed, collecting admissions at the gate; emptying trash cans; picking up in the cluttered dressing rooms after untidy visitors, who invariably threw paper towels on the floor instead of into wastebaskets; and refilling empty pop machines with freshly iced bottles from the refrigerator. Auntie Casey had never asked them to work, but when they had seen how busy she was, with only Mildred to help out, they had assumed the responsibility voluntarily.

By Monday, however, everything was calm once more. The pool was drained, scrubbed out, and refilled from the pipes leading to the river. That took a whole day, and ordinarily it left the twins with nothing to do, but this morning Joey came up with an idea. He had been mulling it over most of the weekend, for in a way it was a little scary, but he had decided it was the only thing to do.

"I think we ought to go see Huck today," he informed Joan as soon as they had finished breakfast. "Maybe Auntie Casey will let us make a picnic, and we can ask him to eat with us."

"You mean go to his house?" Joan's mouth made a red O of alarm.

"He came to ours."

"I know, but his grandfather! Mildred says he's crazy. I don't think Auntie Casey would like us to go where there's a crazy man. Besides, I'd be scared," she finished honestly.

"We don't know for sure that he is," argued Joey. He had been all over this in his own mind. "She said there was something wrong with Huck, too, and we know that isn't so. Besides, Huck wouldn't let his grandfather hurt us."

"Huck isn't very big. He's not even as big as we are. What could he do?"

"We can always run," Joey insisted. "Huck's grandfather is supposed to be old, so he couldn't run very fast. Besides, I don't think we'd have to. We'd be very polite, and there's no reason why he should chase us."

"If we just had somebody big along," Joan hesitated.

"We can take George!" declared Joey, wondering why he hadn't thought of it before. "Of course, he won't come up very close. He wouldn't want Huck's grandfather to see him. But we'll get him to wait where he can hear us yell if we need him. George wouldn't let anything happen to us, and you know it."

"If you're sure that George will go, too." Joan gave in, as he was sure she would. "But we'll have to ask Auntie Casey."

Obviously Auntie Casey had never heard any of

94

the stories about Huck's grandfather, for she thought it was a splendid idea.

"Lily said that poor child doesn't have many friends," she remembered. "It would be nice to ask him to a picnic. The river's low, but why don't you take fish poles and try your luck? I haven't taken out a family permit this season to fish on the reservation, but you could get one for the day. Give the money to Huck's grandfather. He can turn it over to the Tribal Council, or whatever it is they do with it."

She gave Joey fifty cents from her purse and helped Joan fill a basket with lunch. Then she declared that it was a good time to work on her accounts, since the house would be quiet. The twins were delighted to see the ledgers and pencils and cashbox laid out on the breakfast table. Keeping books required deep concentration on Auntie Casey's part. She wouldn't even think about them again until late afternoon.

George came padding down the cliff at their first call, his spiked tail wagging joyously.

"My dear friends," he exclaimed. "How nice of you to come. I was beginning to feel neglected."

"We couldn't come before," explained Joan quickly. "We had to help our Auntie Casey. But we'll make up for it today. We've brought a picnic."

"A picnic?" The great tail missed a beat, and the stegosaurus stepped forward anxiously. "A picnic doesn't mean strangers, does it? You haven't brought outsiders here, as that naughty Huck did?"

"Of course not," Joan assured him. "A picnic is food. Good things to eat. You eat them outdoors."

"That's where I always eat," George decided thoughtfully. "So that must make all my meals picnics."

"Not quite. Because at picnics you invite friends to eat with you. Good friends, like you and us and Huck. We brought the food in that basket, and we want you to go with us while we get Huck."

"Perhaps I had better wait here," suggested George. "I've been close to the cave where Huck lives. There's another mammal sharing it with him. I was quite safe at that time, because it was night. Even through the walls of the cave I could hear the sounds of sleeping. But with the sun shining, the mammal might be awake. I shouldn't care to run the risk of his catching sight of me."

"It wouldn't be a picnic for you to eat here," said

Joan. "It's not a picnic unless you go somewhere else to eat it."

"You're sure that's necessary?" George's beady black eyes regarded them intently. "Of course, I've never heard of a picnic, so I don't understand any of the rules. But it does seem rather silly to go somewhere else when we have such a nice place as this, complete with hot drinking water."

"Anyway, we're going fishing afterwards," said Joey.

"Fishing?"

"A fish is a creature that lives only in the water," explained Joan. "You must have seen fish, George."

"Although I prefer to live on land, I know a little about creatures who live only in water," admitted George. "Ichthyosaurus does, and Leptolepis, and, of course,

Plesiosaurus, although there has to be quite a bit of water for Plesiosaurus. More than there is around here. He's a sea serpent, you know."

"We'll show you what fishing is when we get there," promised Joey. "And you don't have to go clear up to the house with us. You can hide close by while we get Huck."

"Very close by," emphasized Joan. "Close enough so you can hear us."

"Very well," decided George bravely. "But I do hope the picnic will be all you say it is."

"Peanut butter and jelly sandwiches," Joan told him. "And carrot sticks and cookies and oranges."

"I don't believe I have ever tasted any of those things," decided the stegosaurus. "I do wish you had brought bananas. They're my favorite."

"We'll bring you a banana just as soon as they get some at the store," promised Joey. "Come on. Let's get going."

He led the way, and the others followed. Although the land looked flat, it had a tendency to roll slightly, and the old road was like a loose piece of string tossed down on a rough surface. It did not run in a straight line but straggled along, sometimes disappearing completely behind a stand of sage. The river was not more than a mile away, but it ran below, in the same deep gorge which contained Auntie Casey's summer resort, leaving the rimrock-encircled stretch on which they walked dry and barren except for the sage.

George enjoyed the sage. He paddled along on his cumbersome feet, pausing now and then to nibble at any clump which grew too close to the road. Joan always stopped when he did, waiting patiently until he was ready to go on, but Joey soon was far ahead.

"Hurry up, George," he shouted, looking over his shoulder. "You'll spoil your picnic by eating beforehand."

"I don't think there's much chance of that," observed George mildly. "It's a very small basket."

Although she did not say so, Joan, who was taking her turn just then at carrying the lunch, could hardly agree. The basket was heavy, for Auntie Casey had been liberal. There was far more than three children could eat. But, of course, Auntie Casey hadn't known it would be shared by a stegosaurus.

After they had walked for what seemed to the twins a very long way, George stopped.

"I'm not going any farther," he announced. "It isn't safe. Huck's cave is just ahead."

Rising above the sagebrush was the rough shape of a gray rooftop. It was necessary to look closely, for it was a small roof and almost lost against the grayish-brown cliffs.

"Just a little farther," pleaded Joan.

But the stegosaurus was firm.

"No," he declared. "This is quite close enough. The wind is blowing me the scent of mammals. I smell both horse and man. Huck's cave is only about six Tyrannosaurus-leaps away. Besides, the sagebrush here has a delicious flavor. It will make a nice appetizer for the picnic."

Although they did their best, they were unable to coax him any closer, and finally they had to go on alone.

"Maybe we ought to go back." Joan was worried. "I'm scared of Huck's grandfather."

"If we want to help Huck, we have to go," Joey reminded her. "We can't expect him to come to our house all the time. Besides, if the wind can blow smells to George, it will blow sounds, too. He'll hear us if we call for help."

"But would he come?" shivered Joan.

"Maybe not if he had time to think about it beforehand," replied Joey seriously. "But if he heard us yell that we were in danger, I think he'd come running to save us without even stopping to remember he was shy."

They could see the house quite plainly by this time, and at first they thought George had made a mistake. Surely Huck didn't live there. The house gave the appearance of having been deserted long ago. It was a shack, and so in need of repair that it looked as though a strong wind might blow it away. The walls and patched roof were gray and weathered, for the splintery boards had never been finished or painted, and the whole thing sagged tipsily. Some of the small windows were broken out, and the openings were patched up with old boards. A stone chimney veered off to an angle, as though it was beginning to lose its battle against the elements.

Behind the house was a second building in an even more sorry state of repair. It must have been a barn, for it was connected with a fenced corral, in which stood a dejected, white-and-black-spotted horse.

The twins gave only a brief inspection to any of these things. Instead, they concentrated on an old wagon which had been pulled up on the opposite side from the corral. A boy was standing in the wagon bed, throwing rough lengths of wood onto a rapidly mounting pile on the ground.

"It's the right place," said Joey in relief. "There's Huck."

"Where's his grandfather?" whispered Joan nervously.

"He's not there." Joey lifted his voice and called out joyfully, "Huck! Hey, Huck! We came to take you to a picnic."

CHAPTER *TEN*

HUCK HAD NOT WANTED
his grandfather to go back to the mountains for more
firewood after only one day of rest, but he had been
unable to stop him. Opalo was determined. This morning after their return, he was so tired that he hadn't
even suggested that he would help unload the wagon.
He had picked at his breakfast of cold bread and hot
root tea; then he had gone wearily back to his bed.
He was old, he said, and the old were good for nothing; perhaps the young men on the reservation were
right and he had outlived his usefulness.

It made Huck feel strange and miserable to hear his
grandfather say such things. Opalo had never before
admitted that he was growing feeble. When he had
spoken of his age, it had been with pride. Additional
years brought greater wisdom. Besides, a medicine
man did not require great physical strength.

But lately, Huck suddenly realized, his grandfather
seldom reminded anyone of his calling. Perhaps he was
beginning to accept the fact that the young tribesmen no longer believed in such things and that medicine men had been discarded with the customs of taking scalps and wearing war paint. Of course, if Opalo
didn't talk about his powers, people wouldn't think him
peculiar, but somehow that didn't seem so important
today as it had before. Huck wanted his grandfather
to be happy, and he certainly wasn't that.

Although he, too, was tired, he had started unloading the second wagon immediately. There had been no time to stack the first load properly, and now the second was being thrown down on top of that. Huck would have preferred to leave the whole thing and spend the day with his new friends, Joey and Joan—to swim in that beautiful blue tiled pool and afterwards walk up and visit with George. But it didn't seem quite right to be off enjoying himself while his grandfather stayed alone. Opalo was worried about the wood for winter. Perhaps it would be comforting to know that the work was continuing while he rested.

Huck tried to forget about his sore back and aching muscles by thinking of his new friends. How fine it was to have friends, even though one of them had to be kept a secret. Very few people in the world could claim a live stegosaurus for a friend, so it was quite a distinction. He did wish, though, that George would get over some of his odd notions. Imagine anyone thinking that he, Huck, needed to be looked after! Why, he had been on his own almost since he could remember. Grandfather generally let him do as he pleased, and at school, so long as he did his lessons and obeyed the rules, the teachers left him alone. The students left him alone, too, but that was for a different reason. They thought he was queer. But Joey and Joan and George didn't think he was queer. They liked him.

He paused to wipe perspiration from his streaming face, and it was then that he heard someone calling to him.

"Huck! Hey, Huck! We came to take you to a picnic!"

He whirled around, startled, and there were Joey and Joan coming down the road. For the first time he was glad that his grandfather had been tired enough to go back to bed. Opalo did not encourage visitors. Huck jumped down from the wagon and ran to meet them.

"What are you doing?" cried Joey eagerly. "Where have you been? We thought you'd be back to swim."

"I couldn't," explained Huck. He saw that Joan was sagging under the heavy basket, and he reached over to help her carry it. "I had to go to the mountains after firewood. I'm unloading it now."

"Did you go all by yourself?" asked Joey.

"No. With my grandfather."

"Where is he now?" asked Joan quickly.

"Sleeping," Huck told her. "He's tired. He's very old."

"Would he let you go on a picnic?" asked Joey.

"George is waiting for us back there. He wouldn't

105

come any closer. We thought we could go fishing if we can find a place."

"My grandfather would let me go fishing," nodded Huck. "We could use the fish for supper. But I'll have to finish unloading the wagon first."

"We'll help you," volunteered Joey. "You'll get through faster."

Joey and Huck climbed up into the wagon, and both began throwing limbs onto the ground. Joan wanted to help, too, but when her brother insisted that there wasn't room in the wagon for three people and all the wood, she began gathering up scattered sticks from the ground and stacking them in a neat pile.

"That's a big help," called Huck gratefully. "It's the part I hate most."

"I don't mind doing it," said Joan obligingly.

With two of them working, the wagon was emptied swiftly. It was almost like a game to see who could throw down the most, but suddenly Huck realized that Joey had straightened up, the stick which he had been ready to toss onto the heap still in his hand. His eyes were round and a little anxious, and the smile had faded from his face.

Huck turned quickly. His grandfather was standing on the ground, a little beyond the beginning of the woodpile. His gray head, with the long braids falling over the shoulders of his ragged shirt, was bare, and his sharp-featured face was stern. He was not angry—not as he had been the day in the parking lot when he frightened Nappy and Bob—but he didn't look very friendly either.

"Weewino," he called harshly in Klickitat. "Who are these whites? What do they do here on our land?"

Huck swallowed. Grandfather was preparing to send Joey and Joan home. He was going to tell them that strangers were not welcome here. It was more than he could bear.

"These are my friends, Grandfather," he answered in Klickitat, and the sound of his own voice seemed to give him a little courage. "They are the only friends I have. At school I have no friends. Everyone thinks I am strange. Sometimes they laugh at me, and I hear them. But these two white children do not laugh. They want my friendship, and they give me theirs. They have entertained me in their lodge. Are you going to stop me from returning their hospitality?"

For a long moment after Huck had finished speaking, Opalo was silent. His face was set and serious, but his eyes weren't quite so stern.

"No," he said finally. "If they are your friends, I shall not send them away, Weewino. But it is strange that the great-grandson of Opalo must turn to the whites for friendship. What are their names?"

Huck began to smile. It was a small expression of the great happiness he felt inside him. Grandfather was going to be polite to his guests! He tugged at Joey's arm as a signal to follow when he jumped to the ground.

"This is Joan, Grandfather," he introduced proudly. "And her brother, Joey." Speaking to the twins, he used English. "This is my grandfather, Opalo. I just told him who you are, and he makes you welcome."

"Hello, sir," said Joey cautiously.

"Hello," echoed Joan, who had been cowering against her neat stack of firewood.

Opalo inclined his gray head slightly, looking from one twin to the other.

"The squaw has hair the color of firelight," he observed. "Once, when I was a young man, I saw a scalp that color. It was much prized, although it was old and almost worn out."

"My grandfather says you have pretty hair," Huck told Joan. He was glad she could not understand Klickitat.

"Tell him thank you," she said, smiling faintly.

"A squaw with hair that color would have brought many horses once," continued Opalo thoughtfully. "Our people would never have been so foolish as to take her scalp."

"What did he say then?" demanded Joey.

"He wonders what we can do to entertain you," improvised Huck hastily. He did wish his grandfather would stop staring at Joan's red pigtails.

"Oh," remembered Joey, fishing in his pocket for Auntie Casey's fifty-cent piece. "We're supposed to pay to fish on the reservation. Ask your grandfather if it would be all right and if he'd give the money to whoever is supposed to have it."

Huck took the silver coin and handed it to his grandfather, who promptly put it in his mouth and bit down to make sure it was sound.

"My white friend, Joey, has brought a present to my grandfather," he explained in Klickitat. "He wishes to be friends with him, too."

Opalo put the coin in the pocket of his old pants.

"The present is accepted," he said gravely.

"Grandfather says he'll take care of everything," Huck assured the twins brightly. He knew that he wasn't being legal about it, but no one would see them where he meant to fish, and Opalo would think it discourteous if guests didn't bring a gift on their first visit. "He'll see that the money gets where it's supposed to go."

"I think your grandfather ought to have something from the picnic," said Joan suddenly. "It isn't fair that he has to stay here all alone while we're having fun."

She walked over to where they had set the lunch basket on the ground and rummaged around under the white cloth until she had found one of the oranges. When she held it out to Opalo, the thin brown hand closed on it greedily.

"Joan also wants to make a present to my grandfather," said Huck. He could hardly believe his eyes as he saw the sharp old face break into a reluctant smile. "It is another kind of fruit from the land that has no snow."

"I accept this present also," said Opalo graciously. "Tell them they are welcome in my lodge and that they may come again."

This time the translation which Huck made into English was accurate, and he was delighted to see his friends and his grandfather exchange guarded smiles.

"Is it all right if we all go fishing, Grandfather?" he asked. "We haven't anything to eat but flour."

"Go," nodded Opalo. "And check the traps on your return. There may be a rabbit in one of them."

Huck told the twins that they had better leave right

away. He used the excuse that at this time of day they would need all their skill to tempt a fish to take a hook, but actually he wanted to go while everyone was smiling.

"Tell your grandfather we're glad we met him," said Joan properly.

"And tell him I've always wanted to meet a real medicine man," added Joey. "I think it's swell that I finally did."

Huck looked at him quickly. He hadn't known that the twins knew his grandfather was a medicine man. Could it be that they were laughing at him? But Joey's face was perfectly serious. He meant what he said.

"My friends say they are glad that they met you, Grandfather," he translated. "And Joey says to tell you he has always wanted to meet a real medicine man. He is proud that he finally did."

Opalo had just bitten into the orange, but he stopped. His eyes looked as sharply into Joey's face as Huck's had done, and he apparently approved of what he saw. Although he did not speak, his shoulders straightened and he nodded a proud acknowledgment. Huck couldn't help sensing that his grandfather was happier than he had been for days.

CHAPTER *ELEVEN*

ALTHOUGH THE WARM SPRINGS RIVER ran adjacent to the acres belonging to Opalo, its waters had never been utilized to their fullest extent. Here no pipes or irrigation ditches led out from the stream, as they did in sections belonging to progressive farmers. The river was allowed to continue onward in its ancient course to join the larger Deschutes, just as it had always done. At this point there was no gorge carved in the rocky cliffs, no deep bed between timbered slopes. The stream sprawled widely, shallowly, over small boulders and through gravel, and in the low of summer the water shrank, leaving rock-studded beaches on either side. It looked more like a creek than a real river. Most anglers would have bypassed this section entirely, but Huck knew that there were often trout lurking in some of the deeper pools, and here was where he led his friends.

"I feel dreadfully exposed," protested George plaintively. "I shall never have a comfortable moment here."

"There's nobody around but us," Joan assured him.

"And nobody else ever comes here," added Huck. "You're perfectly safe."

George sniffed loudly, turning his huge body in every direction.

"I don't smell mammals," he admitted. "Except you

three. But I shall certainly have to be on my guard."

"Let's eat," suggested Joey, changing the subject. "I'm starved."

Joan took the white cloth from the basket and spread it on the rocky ground.

"Is that part of the picnic?" asked George, watching her intently.

"It's the tablecloth. Of course, we don't have any table, but you often don't at picnics."

George stepped closer and sniffed one corner.

"There's a certain fragrance," he admitted. "But I'm not sure it's edible. It might be hard to chew."

"You never eat the tablecloth," Joey told him hastily. "Only the things you put on it."

The stegosaurus watched critically as Joan set out the food, a tall stack of sandwiches, a heap of cookies, sliced carrots in a waxed-paper bag, and two oranges.

"It's just as well that I nibbled a little on the way," he observed.

Joey agreed silently. It had seemed like a great deal of lunch when they started, for Auntie Casey had made nine sandwiches, three apiece; but spread out on the cloth, it didn't seem so much. Not when it had to be shared with anyone so huge as George. Joey wished that Joan hadn't insisted on giving one of the oranges to Huck's grandfather.

"The sagebrush begins only a little way back there," said Huck sensibly. "If you're still hungry after lunch."

"True." George brightened. "I sampled it on the way down. It was quite luscious, too."

"Help yourselves," invited Joan hospitably. "George, let me give you a sandwich."

"A sandwich isn't meat, is it?" The stegosaurus hesitated delicately. "Don't forget that I'm a vegetarian."

"This is peanut butter and jelly," she assured him, unfolding the wax paper. "No meat at all."

The whole sandwich disappeared into his mouth at one time, and George chewed twice before he swallowed.

"A foreign taste," he decided. "Probably one that must be acquired."

"Didn't you like it?" asked Joey a little hopefully. So long as George liked sagebrush, there was really no need in wasting perfectly good sandwiches on him.

"I shall acquire the taste," declared George determinedly. "Another bite, please, Joan."

She dutifully unwrapped a second sandwich, which vanished as quickly as the first. Joey began to eat as fast as he could. He saw that Huck was doing the same thing, but poor Joan was kept so busy supplying George that she managed only to take a few bites from her own sandwich.

"I do believe I've done it," declared George finally. "It was difficult, but I've acquired the taste for sandwiches."

"Now that they're all gone," said Joey significantly. He and Huck had only finished one apiece in the time it had taken the stegosaurus to devour six. He saw Joan hastily stuff the remainder of hers into her mouth.

"What's next?" asked George brightly. "I'm game to try anything but meat."

"Carrot sticks," mumbled Joan through the last of her sandwich.

This time she was wiser. She divided the contents

of the waxed-paper bag into four equal piles before offering George his share.

George liked carrots well enough, although he confessed that he really considered them inferior to sagebrush as a steady diet, and he smacked his lips so loudly over his share of the cookies that Joan divided hers with him. The cloth was now bare except for the two oranges.

"Is that dessert?" asked George. "They look rather like yellow eggs. Why didn't you bring one for everybody?"

"They're oranges," explained Joan. "Only I don't get any. I gave mine to Huck's grandfather."

"You can eat mine, Joan," said Huck quickly. "I don't like oranges too well anyway."

"Why don't we divide them up?" suggested Joey. He was still hungry, but he had seen Huck eyeing the fruit. Huck wasn't telling the truth when he said he didn't like oranges.

"That wouldn't be fair when I gave mine away." Joan shook her head so violently that her red braids stood out on each side. "I won't eat a bite."

"Neither will I," said Huck stubbornly.

"Very well," agreed George. "That leaves one apiece for you and me, Joey."

"You can eat them both," Joey said angrily. It wasn't fair of Joan and Huck to act this way. It made him seem like a selfish pig.

"Thank you."

To Joey's surprise, George accepted instantly. The long neck craned over the white cloth, and the rough head bent over the oranges. There were two loud snaps,

and when the stegosaurus resumed his former position, the cloth was bare. Slowly, methodically, the jaws moved with a chewing motion, and George swallowed thoughtfully.

"You were all quite right in refusing dessert," he declared finally. "This fruit is sour, and the skin is distinctly bitter. What is the next thing we do at a picnic?"

"We're going fishing," said Joey shortly. He stood up and walked over to where he had left his creel. "We brought worms, Huck, if you want to use some."

Huck shook his head.

"Let's see if they're feeding first," he said. "They usually don't this time of day. But sometimes there's been a bug hatch, and when that happens we may be lucky."

He walked out on the rocks, studying the white-riffled water, which seemed to be pushing only half-heartedly on its course. Here and there a few brave bushes grew along the shore, their green boughs stretched out over the stream, and Huck inspected these also.

"Caddis flies," he called triumphantly. "That's what we want for bait. By evening the fish will really set to and bite, but maybe we can pick up a few greedy ones now."

"Fish," repeated George thoughtfully. "Fish live in water. You intend to take them out? For food?"

"People do eat fish," agreed Joan a little reluctantly.

"Barbarous," sighed George. "Of course, I shan't try to stop you, since it's your nature. But I don't care to

116

watch. I'll run up for a little sagebrush while I'm waiting."

"We aren't going to eat them now," Joey protested.
"We don't eat them raw."

But George didn't hear. He was already padding
back across the rocks to the drier area above.

Huck was right. It was the wrong time of day to do
much fishing, and if he hadn't managed to lure two
trout from under their hiding places beneath rocky
ledges, Joey would never have believed there was a fish
in this part of the river. Neither he nor Joan had so
much as a nibble, and he was very disappointed.

"You may have these," said Huck politely, but Joey
refused to take them. Somehow he couldn't help feeling that Huck and his grandfather needed the fish for
food.

"But it's no fun fishing when they don't bite," he
confessed. "I wish there was something else to do."

"So do I," agreed Joan in a worried tone. "Something
that would be fun for George. We told him a picnic
was fun, and he isn't having any."

"He's eating, isn't he?" demanded Joey pointedly.
"And he got most of the lunch. That ought to make
him feel good."

"I know what you mean," said Huck slowly. "It's no
fun to be by yourself all the time. We ought to do something with him."

"Maybe we could play a game," suggested Joan. "But
it ought to be something he could win."

"You mean every time?" demanded Joey in surprise.

"Every time," she repeated flatly. "After all, we
promised him a good time."

"Yes, we did," agreed Joey honestly. His freckled forehead twisted into a frown as he tried to concentrate. "What kind of games do they play at picnics anyway? There's baseball."

"George would never understand baseball," declared Joan. "Besides, there aren't enough of us."

"Races?" offered Huck tentatively.

Joey shook his head.

"He can beat us getting up and down cliffs but not on a straightaway. He'd forget what he was doing and stop to eat sagebrush."

"Run, sheep, run?" suggested Joan. "Blindman's buff? Tag?"

"Not if you want to be sure he wins." Joey rejected every suggestion with a shake of his head.

"I know," declared Huck, and his black eyes shone. "Indian wrestling. George can't help but win at that."

"We don't know how," said Joan.

"It's a game of strength," Huck told her. "And you know George is strong. Come on, let's go tell him."

They found the stegosaurus calmly finishing off what had once been a sizable clump of sage.

"Is the picnic over?" he asked, turning to regard them with his bright-black eyes. "Have you satisfied your carnivorous appetites?"

"We caught two fish," said Huck, holding up the string. "But we didn't eat them. Here they are."

"They're Leptolepis!" exclaimed George. "Why didn't you call them by their right name? I'm delighted that you changed your mind about eating them. Let me recommend a little of this sage instead."

"We aren't at all hungry," fibbed Joey. "And we

thought it was time to get on with another part of the picnic. The games."

"Games?" repeated George suspiciously. "What are games?"

"That's what you do on a picnic for fun," explained Joan.

"The game we're going to play is Indian wrestling," said Huck. "It's a game to see who is strongest. I'm the only one who knows how to play it, so I'll show you all. First I'll wrestle Joey. Then the winner will wrestle Joan, and the winner of that will wrestle you."

"Why do I have to be last?" asked George in an injured tone.

"Oh, you don't," cried Joan quickly. "Would you rather be first?"

"No," decided George after a moment. "I just wanted to make sure I could be if I wanted to. I prefer to be last. It's more courteous."

"All right, Joey," said Huck quickly before the stegosaurus had time to reconsider. "You stand there on this line." He marked off two parallel scratches on the ground with the toe of his ragged shoe. "And I'll stand on this one. Now we join hands and touch elbows. That's all we can touch, remember. You try to throw me over onto the ground, and I'll try to throw you. But don't move off the line."

Joey stood on the line and took Huck's hard little hand in his own. Their fingers interlaced, and their arms pressed close together to the elbows. Huck was shorter and slighter, but Joey could feel that the small arm against his own was hard. He strained and pushed, but it did not give an inch. Then suddenly, almost before he knew what was happening, he felt his own arm bend and his body sway. He staggered to keep his balance, and Huck let go.

"You lost," he said almost apologetically. "You stepped off the line."

"Let me try again," cried Joey eagerly. "I think I can do it this time. I didn't know what to look for."

"No, you don't," objected Joan firmly. "One turn apiece. It's mine now. Unless you want to go first, George?"

"No, no," objected the stegosaurus. "I'll watch again. But I think I'm getting the idea."

Huck had Joan's feet off the line almost immediately, and she stepped back, laughing in her defeat.

"It's harder than it looks, George," she warned. "Be careful."

"Oh, I will," he promised in a worried tone. "But I've never played a game before, so I don't expect to win."

With George as a contestant, they found that it was necessary to draw new lines and make them farther apart. Although his front legs were short for the rest of his body, when one was extended straight ahead, it covered considerable ground.

"And, of course, I cannot bend my elbow," he explained sadly, "since I have none."

"That's all right, George," Joey reassured him. "The bottom of your foot is just about the same length as our arms anyway."

"So it is," agreed the stegosaurus happily. He lifted his left foot, and upon discovering that he wobbled a little on three, he braced himself with his spiked tail.

"Do you consider this fair?" he asked anxiously. "I wouldn't care to take advantage, just because you aren't lucky enough to have tails."

"Of course it's fair," said Huck. "Ready, set, push!"

Almost before he had said the last word, he tumbled to the ground in a heap. George stared down at him anxiously.

"What happened?"

"Why, you won!" cried Huck, getting to his feet. "You pushed me over in nothing flat."

"But I hardly pushed at all," declared George. "Just the tiniest little nudge."

"That's because you're so strong," Joan assured him. "You don't even know your own strength, George. Why, I bet you could beat anybody in the whole world in Indian wrestling."

"You sure could," said Joey. "You're the champion."

"You make me very happy," confided the stegosaurus. "I can't thank you enough. I've had a wonderful day, and I dearly love picnics. Would anyone care to Indian-wrestle again?"

CHAPTER *TWELVE*

HUCK WAS FEELING FINE as he said good-bye to the twins and George and started down the familiar old trail which his forefathers' feet had worn between the house and the river. It was late afternoon, and Joan and Joey had said that their Auntie Casey would be worried if they didn't appear soon. Indian wrestling had left George very thirsty, and since he scorned the cool, sweet water in the river, it was necessary for him to return to his hot mineral spring to get a drink.

Huck had considered staying on at the river alone, waiting for sundown, when the fish would start feeding, but that was several hours away. It would be better to go home, check his grandfather's traps on the way, and prepare an early meal. Opalo wouldn't have eaten anything but Joan's orange since breakfast, and he would be hungry. Huck could come back to the river later on, when he was sure of success.

It had been a wonderful day, and he was grateful for so many things—for the companionship of his three friends and because his grandfather seemed willing to accept the twins, even though they were strangers and white. He was grateful for the two fish, for they meant tonight's supper, and for the bug hatch, which meant that he would catch more for tomorrow.

It was a little disappointing to find there was nothing

in any of the traps, but it didn't matter too much, since they had the trout. Probably it was better this way. If they had fresh meat and fish both, Opalo would have made him spend all tomorrow smoking trout. Huck would have had to tend fires and keep turning the strips of fish in the smoke, so that they would dry to a preserved state for winter's use. And Huck had other plans for tomorrow. He was going back to the pool to swim with Joey and Joan. He was going early and staying for lunch. Auntie Casey had sent him a special invitation.

As he neared the house, his feeling of contentment vanished and he began to run. Above the sage, he caught a glimpse of scarlet streaking along the road from the agency—a color strangely out of place in the gray and brown landscape. It could only be the shiny body of an automobile, and so far as Huck knew, there was only one car that shade on the reservation. It belonged to Chief Charley Whitewater.

As he raced along, he prayed that he would arrive before the car. Chief Whitewater had plans to move Opalo away from his acres, into an agency which had only disdain or pity for the old man. Huck had to be there when the chief arrived, to show him that his grandfather wasn't completely alone and friendless.

He made it, panting and almost speechless, just as the car drove up in front. Chief Whitewater was driving, and Dr. Mercer was sitting beside him.

"Hello, Huck," called the chief. His black eyes took in the two trout hanging from a line in the boy's hand. "Been fishing? They bite better at sundown."

"I know," gasped Huck. "I'll go back."

"Takes a mighty smart fisherman to get them to rise to a fly this time of day," praised Dr. Mercer. "Or did you use a fly, Huck?"

"Caddis," he said, and saw the doctor smile a little ruefully. He knew it was because sportsmen used only artificial flies, not the real insects. But sportsmen didn't depend on their catches for food.

"We'd like to see your grandfather, Huck." Chief Whitewater opened the car door and stepped out. He had recently been to a barbershop, and there was a paler streak between his sunburned neck and the line of black hair. He wore a short-sleeved sport shirt, crisply creased slacks, and polished black leather loafers.

"I think he's sleeping," Huck told him quickly. "He's tired today. Yesterday we went to the mountains for firewood. It's a long trip."

The chief's eyes moved over the huge pile of fir, still scattered on the ground at the end of the wagon.

"You ought to talk to me first, Huck, before you do anything like that," he chided. "There are places where it's perfectly all right to help yourself to a load, particularly small stuff like that. But there are other places on the reservation where you'd be trespassing. You could get into bad trouble."

"This land belongs to our people, and everything on it is ours, Charley Whitewater," said a stern voice from the open doorway of the house. A moment later, Opalo stepped outside. "We are not trespassers, and we take nothing that does not belong to us."

The chief had spoken to Huck in English, yet Opalo, who addressed him in Klickitat, had understood everything he had said. Huck realized that what he had always suspected was true; his grandfather could speak English if he wanted to. He wondered, momentarily, how much of the conversation with Joey and Joan he had comprehended.

"Hello, Opalo," greeted Chief Whitewater cheerfully. "Glad to see you. You know Doc Mercer, don't you?"

The doctor had climbed out of the car, and now he walked over to the old man and extended his hand. Opalo ignored it completely. Huck's face burned with embarrassment, but Dr. Mercer didn't seem upset. He only smiled and let his hand fall to his side.

"What do you want here, Charley Whitewater?" asked Opalo gruffly.

The chief's round face wrinkled thoughtfully as he turned to Huck.

"I'm not quite sure, but I think he asked me what I wanted. I used to know quite a few words of Warm Springs when I was a kid, but I've almost forgotten them. My grandmother talks it once in a while, but nobody else around the place understands, so she's about given it up."

"He asked what you wanted," said Huck.

"Tell him I've been worried about him," said the chief promptly. "About his health. It's my duty to look after my people, and I've brought Doc Mercer here to check your grandfather over and make sure he's all right."

Although he was sure that his grandfather understood, Huck repeated the chief's message in Klickitat.

"Remind him that I am myself a medicine man," replied Opalo haughtily when Huck had finished. "The spirits will speak to me directly. I do not need to employ the services of another medicine man."

"Grandfather says thank you," said Huck. "But he feels just fine. He doesn't want to bother Dr. Mercer."

"No bother." Dr. Mercer smiled, reaching for his bag on the seat of the car.

"He's paid to do it," grinned the chief. "His services are free."

"Tell them what I said," ordered Opalo, glaring at his grandson. "Use my words, not yours. Yours are weak. They are woman-words. It is not fitting that Opalo should speak such words."

"Grandfather says he is a medicine man himself," repeated Huck unhappily. He wished that his grandfather would just submit to an examination and let things ride. "He says the spirits speak to him. He doesn't need another medicine man."

"Now, Huck," frowned the chief. "That's rubbish and you know it. All we want him to do is let Doc check his heart and blood pressure. Make a few tests. Your grandfather's an old man."

"Tell him that my heart is strong," ordered Opalo coldly. "The spirits have told me so. They are my protectors. They come to me in visions and warn me of my enemies. Now that I am old, my enemies think to discredit me. But the spirits will discredit my enemies."

"What did he say?" frowned the chief, and when Huck had reluctantly repeated the speech, he sighed. "I'd hate to think that what people have been saying about the old man is true, Doc."

"Oh, let's not be hasty," objected Dr. Mercer. "He's old, yes. And his mind wanders a little. But that's to be expected. I would like to check his blood pressure, though. He shouldn't be doing heavy work."

"He's not going to be doing heavy work," promised the chief grimly. "I aim to move him into the agency this fall. Huck, ask your grandfather if he wouldn't like to live with some family where there's somebody to take care of him. All he'd have to do would be to sit and take it easy."

"But he's got a family," protested Huck. "He's got me."

"You have to go to school." Dr. Mercer smiled at him encouragingly. "For a few more years, anyway. Then when you're grown and have a house of your own, your grandfather can come and live with you. In the meantime, he could board with a nice family like the Posts——"

"The Posts!" cried Huck in horror.

"It's not charity," put in Chief Whitewater hastily. "There's money to pay. The Tribal Council will see to it. But he shouldn't be living out here alone. He's too old."

"I won't let you!" Huck ran and threw his arms around his grandfather protectingly. "You can't do that to him. You can't send him to the Posts, where he'll be laughed at and made fun of."

"Laughed at?" repeated Dr. Mercer. "Who's laughing?"

"You just got through saying that people talk about him," Huck reminded the chief.

"Oh, some of them do." Chief Whitewater seemed a little embarrassed. "But they'd probably say the same things about my grandmother, Huck, if they weren't afraid of me. They're old, your grandfather and my grandmother, and you can't teach old dogs new tricks. All we want to do is help him."

"It would not help him to send him to live with the Posts," insisted Huck. "Why can't you leave him alone?"

"Because it isn't right," answered the chief stubbornly. "He can't winter here again, Huck. Not alone. As for the Posts, they're worried about him. They came and talked to me about it. They offered to take him in. They're a little hard up and could use the money the Council will pay. But we can find somebody else if they aren't agreeable. Now you tell your grandfather that Doc wants to listen to his heart and see that it's all right."

"No!" Huck shook his head violently. "You can't touch him. I won't let you!"

"I couldn't get a true reading anyway, with everybody all worked up this way, Charley," said Dr. Mercer quietly. "Better let them think it over for a few days. Get used to the idea. Then we'll listen to his heart and take his blood pressure."

"All right." Chief Whitewater wiped his damp face with his handkerchief. "You two think it over, then. But, remember: Opalo can't spend his winters here alone anymore. So there's no need to lay in more wood. Just as soon as the Huckleberry Festival's over, we'll be making other arrangements."

Neither Huck nor his grandfather answered. They stood silently, watching, as the two men got into the car and drove away.

"Do not worry, Weewino," said Opalo when the red automobile had disappeared into the dust. "I will speak to the spirits. They will not let this thing happen. At the time of the Huckleberry Festival, the spirits are always here. Their powers are strongest then. They will not permit disgrace to fall upon one who has served them so faithfully."

"Maybe the spirits have gone away, Grandfather," Huck told him miserably. "Things have changed. You said so yourself."

Huck wondered how much of the English conversation the old man had been able to follow. Certainly he couldn't have understood everything or he wouldn't have been so positive things would turn out all right.

"The spirits will come to the festival," insisted Opalo. "They always come then, for even those who have strayed away from the customs of our people follow the old ways when we give thanks for the harvest. Meanwhile, we will make certain preparations. We will set up my grandfather's tepee."

Huck realized then that Opalo was as worried as he about Chief Whitewater's plans. There was a mystic significance about the tepee which he himself had never been able to understand. It had belonged to Opalo's grandfather, who was also a medicine man and who had crossed the eastern mountains to the great plains beyond to bring back the buffalo hides from which it was made. His fingers had traced the strange symbols in blue and yellow vegetable dye on the tanned hide, designs which were now so faded that it was hard to make them out.

Every year at the time of the Huckleberry Festival, they loaded the tepee poles and the buffalo covering into the back of the wagon and hauled it to He He

Longhouse. There it was set up in a meadow, a little apart from the other canvas tepees and a few modern tents, to provide living quarters for Opalo and his great-grandson during the festivities.

Huck could remember only two occasions when it had been erected here in the yard. Both had been times of dire emergency—when the old chief died and young Charley Whitewater was elected to replace him, and before Opalo had finally consented to allow Huck to attend the agency boarding school. Whether or not there were certain ancient rites connected with the tepee, Huck did not know. He had never seen his grandfather perform any, but, of course, he could have done so at night, for whenever it was standing, Opalo slept

inside, with the flaps tightly closed. But he would not have ordered it set up in the yard had he not considered the present situation serious.

The supporting poles were kept in the barn. They were young ash trees, four or five inches in circumference and ten or twelve feet high, for the tepee of a medicine man had to be of an imposing size. Opalo had hewed the trees himself, years ago. They were not the original supports, for the buffalo hide had outlasted several sets of poles. They fitted into holes already dug in the ground at proper intervals, and there were cunningly cut notches at the upper end which fitted together so that they would hold in place without tying.

Getting the heavy covering over the support was

the hardest part of the job, and more than once Huck thought they would not be able to do it. The other times, his grandfather had been strong enough to do most of the lifting, but today it was largely up to Huck. He had to get an old sawhorse from the barn to stand on to reach the top, and more than once he tumbled off in a great heap of stiff, unpleasant-smelling leather. But he kept at it determinedly, and his grandfather tried to help, seeming to find a reserve supply of hidden strength. Finally the job was done.

Opalo stood back, and his eyes were reverent as he inspected the tepee, rising like a grayish-brown cone against the rimrock cliff.

"It is good to see it standing so," he said softly.

"Are you going to sleep out here tonight, Grandfather?" panted Huck. He threw himself on the ground. Every muscle in his arms and shoulders ached, and his legs were shaking from teetering on the sawhorse.

"Not tonight," decided his grandfather. "Tonight the tepee of my grandfather will be empty. I am an old man, Weewino, and the ground is hard on my bones. I will rest one more night in my own bed. But the spirits will see it standing here, and they will know that soon Opalo will be calling upon them. They will know that the trouble is bad, and they will open their ears to my prayers. They will not let one who has honored them so faithfully go unanswered."

"I hope so, Grandfather," sighed Huck wearily.

He wished there really was such a thing as a good spirit to save them.

CHAPTER *THIRTEEN*

THE SUN WAS NOT YET UP
when Huck awoke the following morning. Only pale
light found its way through the small patched windows of the shack. From the next room, he could hear
rhythmic snores, which told him that his grandfather
was still asleep, so he got up and dressed as quietly
as he could.

His muscles ached from lifting the heavy buffalo hide,
and he wished he could go back to bed and sleep for a
week. But, of course, he couldn't. It had been slow work
erecting the tepee, and by the time they had eaten their
evening meal, it was night. At any other time, Opalo
would have told Huck to fish by torchlight, for the old
man was scornful of a law which prohibited this old Indian custom of catching fish. But perhaps he had realized that his grandson, too, was tired. When Huck suggested that he would prefer getting up early to fishing
then, his grandfather had nodded silent assent. They
had both gone straight to bed.

Now it was another day, and there would be no
breakfast unless Huck could lure it from the river or
unless a rabbit had stumbled into one of the traps during the night.

He opened the door softly, closing it behind him as
he stepped outside. Fresh, sweet smells of morning
rushed to greet him, the scent of sage and of dry soil

refreshed by the night's breeze. It was lighter out here than it had been inside the house, and the world had a pinkish glow, reflected from the eastern sky above the rimrock. In the side yard, the dark outline of the tepee rose like a fat, pointed spire. Remembering how they had struggled with it last night, Huck hoped that when they took it to the meadows at He He Longhouse, his grandfather would not be too proud to accept outside help in setting it up again.

Then, instinctively, he began to run toward it, for before his eyes the supporting poles were giving way. The tepee bulged at the bottom; the straight lines blurred as it lurched from side to side. Huck was halfway across the yard, in his race to save it from tumbling, before he realized that the tepee hadn't moved at all. Only a great grayish-brown shape, which had been crouched indiscernibly in front of it, had moved. George had been standing before the huge tepee, and now he was padding forward.

"I thought you'd never come out!" The stegosaurus spoke in a whistling whisper which sounded a little like rustling grass. "We're all going to have to move. As soon as possible. A new mountain chain is on its way up. Only the first peak is through as yet, but it's sure to be followed by others, and when the smoke and lava starts, everything becomes quite messy."

"Mountain chain?" gasped Huck.

"Oh, it's happened before," George assured him ruefully. "Mountains spring up overnight. And the seas dry up and appear someplace else where they've no business to be at all. And the plants that one is used to don't grow there anymore, so that one has to rearrange one's diet and get used to something else. It's very annoying."

Huck looked around him quickly. Everything was exactly as it had been yesterday. He couldn't see any change.

"I would have left at once, as soon as I saw the first peak," continued George. "But I waited to warn you. Your poor little brain would not have understood these things unless they were explained to you. You might stay on and get caught in the middle."

"I don't see any mountain peak," insisted Huck. "What are you talking about?"

"Over there." George tossed his low-hung head in the direction of the tepee. "I've just been examining it. It's the first new mountain I've ever felt. It's quite tender as yet. Just a shell, really. It hasn't even had time to harden."

"That's no mountain," objected Huck. "It's a tepee. An Indian house. My grandfather and I put it up last night."

"Are you sure?" George retraced his steps and stood sniffing the sides of the tepee suspiciously. "It is the shape of a new rocky mountain. It is the color of a rocky mountain. When I stood against it, I was hidden, wasn't I? Just as I am when I stand against a rocky cliff?"

"Yes," agreed Huck, surprised to realize that this was so. "But it isn't a mountain. It isn't even rock. It's buffalo hide, and the poles are wood. And you can take it down and put it up again wherever you want to. People live in it."

"How convenient!" declared the stegosaurus in admiration. "A movable cave! You didn't think of the idea yourself, did you?"

"Of course not."

"I didn't think so." George smiled. "To think of such a thing requires a larger brain than you and I possess."

"But I could have thought of it," insisted Huck quickly. "If somebody hadn't already thought of it first."

"Tut-tut! Don't be touchy. Not with me, anyway," reproved George. "You'll develop instinct someday, just as I have. Which brings me to the point of my visit, or the point which I was working on until I saw the movable cave and mistook it for a new mountain . . ." He broke off speaking, and the spiked tail began to tap against the ground. The beady eyes were concentrating on the shack behind them.

"Grandfather's in there," explained Huck indifferently. "He's asleep."

"He *was* asleep," corrected the stegosaurus quickly. "He's walking now."

He turned and began padding down the old trail to the river, and Huck hurried after him. If Grandfather was awake, he must hurry to get at his fishing or there would be no breakfast.

George did not stop until he had reached the spot where the trail ran down to the river. Then he stood still, trembling a little, while the spiked tail thumped up and down, tearing small holes in the hard earth.

"That was a close call," he admitted. "We were having such an interesting discussion, I almost forgot about the mammal sleeping in the cave."

"He wouldn't have hurt you," said Huck. It was his turn to take the lead, and he spoke to the stegosaurus over his shoulder as he walked on. "My grandfather wouldn't hurt anyone. He's a good man."

"Perhaps he is," agreed George politely, falling in behind. "But he's a stranger, and I am shy. What are you going to do now?"

"I'm going fishing."

"You mean Leptolepising," corrected the stegosaurus kindly. "You did that yesterday. Why are you doing it again?"

"I only caught two yesterday, and they're gone."

"How strange," said George thoughtfully. "Where do you suppose they went?"

"You were going to tell me something about your instinct," said Huck, hastily changing the subject.

"Was I?"

"It had something to do with your visit this morning." Huck unwound the line from his pole and checked the hook. This was just the right time to fish. With any luck at all, he ought to be able to get a good string.

"Of course," remembered George happily. "It was about yesterday's picnic. I can't think when I had a better time. My instinct is to have another picnic today. That's what I came to tell you. This time, you must let me be the host and provide the refreshments."

"I don't think we can today." Huck cast his line expertly into the center of a deep hole. "Joey's and Joan's Auntie Casey asked me to come over there for lunch and to swim in the pool."

"How dull," declared George. "Unless, of course, you plan to have Indian wrestling, too? Perhaps, if you could manage to get rid of the other mammals, I might join you for lunch. We could Indian-wrestle afterwards. Then it would be a picnic."

"If you mean Mrs. Casey, she has to be there," explained Huck. "It's her house, and she's fixing the lunch."

"There should never be more than four at a picnic," sniffed George.

"That depends on the picnic." Huck began pulling in his line. On the end was a flapping ten-inch trout. "Picnics can be any size. The Huckleberry Festival is sort of like a picnic, and there'll be hundreds of people there."

"You'll run out of food," warned George quickly. "You can never bring enough lunch for so many mammals, and the whole picnic will be spoiled."

"There'll be plenty to eat," laughed Huck. "You never saw so much food as there is at the Huckleberry Festival."

"Nor do I expect to," said George. "I shall stay far, far away from that picnic with so many mammals. Perhaps I will have one of my own on the same day."

"That's a good idea." Huck recast the line into the center of the same small pool. If there was one trout, there might be two.

"I shall have a delicious picnic lunch of sagebrush," planned George enthusiastically, "with hot mineral water to drink. As much as I can hold. Since I'll be eating out of doors, it will be a picnic. Joey says that is important. And after I can hold no more, there'll be Indian wrestling . . ." His voice

faltered and broke off in the midst of the sentence.

Huck looked at him curiously.

"It sounds fine, George," he encouraged.

"No, it doesn't," denied the stegosaurus sadly. "It doesn't sound fine at all. Because I just remembered that if I have a picnic by myself, there'll be no one to Indian-wrestle. And that's what's fun."

"Have your picnic another day then," said Huck absently. He had just felt a second tug on his line, which meant that he had been right about trying the same pool again.

"But that is the point of choosing that day," explained George seriously. "Now that I know about it, it would make me very unhappy to have everyone else enjoying a picnic while I wasn't. You and Joey and Joan will have to come to mine."

"I don't know about them," said Huck. "But I can't come to your picnic if you hold it at the same time as the Huckleberry Festival, George. I have to go to that. It's expected of me."

"I do wish you would hurry and develop your instinct," sighed George. "It would tell you that small, exclusive picnics are much preferable to big ones filled with strangers."

In less than an hour, Huck had caught enough fish for breakfast and supper, too, and he started home. George accompanied him as far as the road.

"I must hurry back to my cave," he confessed. "It makes me nervous to be so far away in the daylight. But do drop by to pay your respects on your way to see our friends."

Looking like a huge boulder which had broken off in jagged cracks from one of the cliffs, he went padding down the road to his favorite hiding place among the rocks.

Opalo had a fire going when Huck returned, and before long the trout were sizzling in a pan. The old man was unusually silent this morning. He answered his grandson absently, and when Huck told him he had been invited to spend the day with the twins, Opalo nodded.

"Go," he said. "I have much to do."

"You aren't going to stack that wood," cried Huck in alarm. "I'll do it tomorrow. I promise."

His grandfather shook his head scornfully. The gesture implied that his business was far more important than stacking firewood. Huck knew then that the old man meant to spend the day pleading for help from the old gods of his people. It was no use telling him that he would be wasting his time, so Huck didn't try. But he hoped that Chief Whitewater and Dr. Mercer wouldn't return and find Opalo at his task or they'd think he really was out of his mind.

Joey and Joan were waiting for him by the pool, and the trunks which he had worn before were on one of the beach chairs.

"But don't change into them now," said Joan quickly. "We told Auntie Casey that we'd all ride in to the store with her. She likes company when she drives."

"Maybe they have some bananas and you can take one back to George on your way home," said Joey. "I don't think he was much impressed by our picnic yesterday."

"Oh, he was," Huck assured them quickly. "He wants to have another one today. He likes the Indian wrestling especially."

"So would I, if I could win every time," decided Joey wisely.

Although it was his inclination to be reserved in the presence of strange adults, Huck lost his shyness with Auntie Casey on the ride in to the agency. She insisted that he sit in the front with her, so they could get better acquainted. The twins, riding behind, hung their chins over the back of the seat, and everyone began talking at once.

Before he knew it, Huck was entering into the spirit of the occasion, answering Auntie Casey's questions and comments as easily as Joey and Joan. He began to feel very much at home, and the warm, happy sense of being a welcome part of a group continued until they drove up before the store.

"My land, what's all the people doing here?" demanded Auntie Casey in surprise as she turned into the parking lot. "We'll be lucky if we find a hole to leave the car in."

"What's going on, Huck?" asked Joey.

Huck shook his head, as much at sea as the others.

A large crowd had collected in front of the store. There were probably fifty people milling around, laughing and chattering in what seemed to be a holiday mood. They were all Indians, and predominantly women and children, although Chief Whitewater must be in attendance, for Huck saw his red automobile in the parking lot.

"Lily will know what's going on," declared Auntie Casey, opening the car door and stepping down to the pavement. "Come on, children."

The crowd let them through good-naturedly, and one or two of the women greeted Auntie Casey by name. Some of them smiled and nodded to Huck, but most of the children only stared in open astonishment to see him with Joey and Joan. He knew them all. They attended the same school.

Lily Franchere was standing in the open doorway. She held open the screen for them to enter, smiling a welcome.

"What's all the excitement, Lily?" asked Auntie Casey. "What's going on?"

"Oh, they're waiting for the women to come back from the mountains to tell us when the huckleberries will be ripe so we can schedule the annual festival," explained Lily. "They left early this morning, and they should be back pretty soon now."

"They left this morning?" cried Huck. "But it will take several days."

"Not this time, Huck. They went in Florence Bigsaw's station wagon. And Florence is a fast driver."

"Martha Whitewater, too?" he gasped, remembering when his grandfather had prophesied that the time would come when the appointed scouts would break with custom and drive to the mountains rather than trudge the long miles on foot.

"It was mainly on Martha's account that they drove," said Lily gently. "She couldn't walk that far, Huck, and it would have broken her heart not to say when the berries would be ripe."

"So the Huckleberry Festival will be soon." Auntie Casey nodded in approval. "Now there's something you'll want to see, children. It's the biggest thing we have around here."

"You mean we get to go?" cried Joey in delight. "What do you do?"

"Huck will tell you all about it." Lily smiled. "And you'll really get to see Indians, Joey. All you want. Even an Indian queen."

"Who?" cried Joan.

"It could be me," Lily told her demurely. "Providing I'm lucky. I'm one of the candidates this year."

"Tell us, Huck," demanded Joey.

"I will later," promised Huck. "It's too long to tell now."

He stood in the open doorway, looking out at the crowd awaiting the arrival of the station wagon filled with official scouts. Old Martha wouldn't have liked to ride in a car on such an expedition. Huck admitted to himself that it was sensible to drive to the mountains to inspect the ripeness of the berries, but he knew how Martha must feel. He hoped that the other women had let her test the ripeness of the rose hips and the choke-cherries, that they hadn't let her see them fingering the huckleberries themselves.

A cheer started up outside, and he knew that the station wagon had been sighted on the highway. He went outside on the porch, only half aware that Joey and Joan had followed him.

The crowd was so thick on the steps that they could

not see the car after it pulled up below, but they could hear the shrieked announcement.

"Next weekend! The berries are ripening faster than we thought! They'll be at their best next weekend! We can have the festival then."

Everyone began to cheer and talk at once. Next weekend was very close. There wasn't much time. Word must be sent to guests. Preparations must be made. The wild horses must be brought in for the rodeo and the Longhouse prepared for the ceremony. There was much to do and less time than they had thought to do it in.

Huck saw Chief Whitewater's tall hat dipping down the steps, and he realized that the chief must be going to escort his grandmother to his own car in the parking lot. He ran along the porch, squeezed under the railing, and jumped to the ground. There was nothing he could say to Old Martha, but somehow he felt, for his grandfather's sake, that he should speak to her.

After a few minutes, the chief came walking slowly around the side of the building, his arm around his grandmother. Her wrinkled face looked gray in the brilliant sunshine, and even under her bright shawl Huck could see that she was shivering slightly.

"Good day to you, Grandmother-of-the-Chief," he said in Klickitat.

Chief Whitewater frowned slightly.

"My grandmother is ill, Huck," he said curtly. "The trip was too much for her."

But Martha stopped, and her eyes, which had been closed to slits, widened as she inspected Huck carefully.

"You are the great-grandson of Opalo, medicine man

of the Klickitats?" she asked in the Warm Springs tongue.

Huck nodded. He saw the chief look from one to the other in surprise and remembered that he had forgotten how to speak the old language.

"Go home and tell your grandfather that trouble will soon come to our people," ordered Martha harshly. "Tell him that not only did we drive to the mountains, instead of making our way humbly and on foot, but that when we arrived there Florence Bigsaw took a berry in her mouth and chewed it up to determine its ripeness. Tell Opalo that, boy, as soon as you can. He will know what to do!"

CHAPTER *FOURTEEN*

"I WISH THEY DIDN'T have to hold the festival on a weekend," fussed Auntie Casey as they bumped over the unpaved road back to the resort. "Weekends are so busy for us."

"Does that mean we can't go?" cried Joey in alarm.

"No, of course not," said Auntie Casey. "I'll manage alone. I did before you two came to visit. I wouldn't have you miss the festival for the world."

"I don't think we should go," said Joan slowly. "We ought to stay and help you."

"Nonsense," overruled Auntie Casey. "Now, Huck, you tell us all about it. I've had the festival explained to me, but you can do a better job, I'm sure."

Obediently, Huck told them about the annual festival of the Warm Springs. It was always held in the middle of August, when the berries were ripe, and until after the proper religious ceremony had been observed, no member of the tribe was permitted to eat of the fruit. Here he stopped, remembering how Florence Bigsaw had chewed one of the half-ripe berries. No wonder Martha had been angry. Florence had broken another ancient tradition.

"Go on," Joey reminded him impatiently.

"Oh," said Huck guiltily. "Well, they have salmon and venison, too, besides the berries, and ever since I can remember they've had other things besides—

bread and cake and melons and coffee. But my grand-father says some of those shouldn't be there. All of the food is supposed to come from our own land. The feast is at noon, in the Longhouse, but in the morning they have the ceremonial dances to give thanks to the Great Spirit for giving us these things."

"A little like our Thanksgiving," said Auntie Casey.

"And in the morning there's a parade," continued Huck. "Everybody who has it wears ceremonial dress."

"Do you have one?" demanded Joey. His voice was so filled with envy that Huck was gratified to admit that he did. Not too many boys his own age owned such clothing. They had to be content with a beaded belt or a feather.

The ancient ceremonial robes were gradually being discarded, leather was deteriorating, beads were breaking loose from their strings, and moths were eating the feather trimmings. But almost every family had at least one costume kept in good repair and handed down for special occasions, so that there were enough to make a creditable showing.

After the feast, there would be games—the stick-throwing game and shoot-the-rabbit—and all kinds of races, including one between the oldest men and women in the tribe.

"And they have a track," continued Huck, warming a little to his subject. "There'll be wild-horse racing, and calf roping, and wild-cow milking, and bronc busting. You know, all the things they have in a rodeo."

"Oh, boy!" Joey's eyes shone with excitement.

"And at night there's the Queen's Ball. But I've never

been to one of those, because I don't know how to dance."

"Me, neither," declared Joey. "And I wouldn't want to."

"I would," said Joan. "Especially if Lily gets to be queen. Wouldn't she make a beautiful one?"

"Very beautiful," agreed Auntie Casey, steering the car into the garage and turning off the motor. "Now if you children want to have a swim before lunch, there's just time. I'm going to start getting it ready right away."

All through lunch they discussed the approaching festival. The twins were very excited at the prospect and could think of nothing else. Any other year, Huck would have looked forward to it, too, but now he kept remembering that as soon as it was over Chief Whitewater meant to move his grandfather away from his old home. For the first time, he wondered what change this would have upon himself. He doubted if he would be allowed to spend summers alone in the shack, but if they expected him to go live with the Posts, he wouldn't do it. He'd run away first!

"I'll just die if we can't go," said Joey again. "We just have to."

"I know you do," Auntie Casey agreed. "And you're going. I can drive you over early Saturday morning, before people start coming here, and pick you up in late afternoon, when they've gone. But we'll have to find someone to keep an eye on you. I just can't turn you loose. Maybe Mildred——"

"Not Mildred!" cried Huck involuntarily. "Please, not one of the Posts!"

"But she knows the children," said Auntie Casey in surprise. "And she's pretty responsible, especially if she knows she's being paid to do something."

"They will be with me," promised Huck. "I will look after them."

"And who will look after you, Huck?" Auntie Casey's eyebrows raised teasingly.

"His grandfather!" Joey told her promptly. "And his grandfather's a medicine man! He'd have a lot more authority than old Mildred ever had."

"My grandfather will look after my friends, too," promised Huck.

"We can't ask a strange man to take on the responsibility of two more children." Auntie Casey frowned.

"He's not strange, Auntie Casey. We know him already," said Joan. "And he's very nice. Besides, we'd be with Huck all the time, so his grandfather wouldn't have anything extra to do."

"You wouldn't have to pay my grandfather," pointed out Huck. "You do not pay for an act of friendship."

"But if he did agree to look after them, I'd want to do something." Auntie Casey was beginning to weaken. "At least give him a little gift."

"What kind of presents does he like, Huck?" asked Joey quickly.

"Any kind of fruit. I took him some bananas as a present," remembered Huck. "He liked those best."

"They haven't had bananas at the store for days," argued Auntie Casey helplessly. "Of course, they might have some in Madras, and we do have to go in there Thursday to buy new tennis shoes for Joey."

"Oh, Auntie Casey!" The twins jumped up and ran around to give her violent hugs.

"Now, now," she protested. "I haven't said yes yet. And neither has Huck's grandfather. He'll have to be consulted first. After all, the responsibility of two extra children may be more than he wants to take on."

"May we walk home with Huck and ask?" cried Joey. "After all, we've got to make plans."

"I suppose it wouldn't hurt to ask him," she agreed thoughtfully. "But, just to play safe, I'll tell Mildred to keep an eye on you, too. Between them, they ought to make sure you're all right for a few hours."

The twins shrieked with delight, but Huck felt a little let down. Joey and Joan were his friends. He didn't want one of the Posts attempting to usurp his privilege of showing them around at the festival.

Instead of spending the afternoon in the pool, as they had planned, they went to consult Opalo. Privately, Huck considered the whole thing rather silly. Twelve-year-olds did not need to be "looked after." They were capable of taking care of themselves. But Auntie Casey had been insistent, and unless an adult agreed to be in charge, the twins would not be allowed to attend the festival.

They waited until she was safely inside the house before they started up the old path along the steep cliff.

"It's just as well not to worry her," explained Joey. "And she might worry if she saw us going up this trail. The other day, when we came to see you, we went around by the road. But it takes a lot longer."

"It was easier, though," remembered Joan. She was carrying two cupcakes left over from lunch, wrapped

separately in waxed paper. One was for George, because he had been disappointed in not having another picnic, and the second was for Huck's grandfather. Huck was especially glad about that one. Opalo considered that frequent gifts were only fitting to a man of his calling.

When they reached the top, they found the stegosaurus waiting for them. He had been standing against the tall rock wall, which extended upward another fifty feet before it ended abruptly in a flat, even surface.

"I thought you were never coming," he said reproachfully, stepping forward so that his jagged shape was discernible. "I've been waiting and waiting."

"I brought you a cupcake," said Joan hastily, unwrapping one of the small packages.

George swallowed the cupcake solemnly, then reopened his mouth, his beady eyes on the second cupcake.

"That's not for you," she explained. "It's a present for Huck's grandfather, because we're going to ask a favor of him."

"Perhaps I could do the favor instead," he suggested. "That was hardly a taste."

"I don't think so," said Joey. "You see, we want to go to the Huckleberry Festival, only Auntie Casey won't let us unless there's a grown-up along who'll look after us. That's what we want Huck's grandfather to do."

"Is that the large picnic with too many mammals and not enough food?" asked George disapprovingly. "You don't want to go to that! Now I happen to know where there'll be another picnic on the same day. A small, exclusive picnic, with more than anyone can eat and plenty of Indian wrestling."

"But we want to go to the Huckleberry Festival, George," said Joey.

"Things like that don't happen very often," added Joan. "It will be fun. And educational, too."

"Besides, there'll be plenty to eat," insisted Huck. "You never saw so much food. There has to be a lot of it, because the tribes camp there for several days."

"Camp?" questioned George.

"You remember the tepee you saw in our yard this morning? The one you thought was a mountain? We'll move it there and live in it until the festival's over. It lasts three days."

"I didn't know that," cried Joey indignantly. "We only asked to go one day."

"Maybe you can come back," suggested Huck. "The first day's the best, anyway."

"Does everyone live in a movable cave?" asked the stegosaurus curiously.

"Sure," said Huck. "You'd really think it was a new mountain range if you saw them all set up on the meadow. Ours is the biggest, though. And it's practically the only one made of real buffalo hide. Most everybody else has just canvas tepees."

"I can hardly wait to see it," confessed Joan. "I wish you could go, too, George."

"I would like to," he admitted grudgingly. "If I were the size of a mouse, I would. Because then I could be sure that I wouldn't have to be embarrassed by meeting strangers. I often stand against the cliff and watch you two and the other mammals down below. You never know that I'm here, so I feel quite safe."

"Maybe there's some rimrock cliffs close to the festival grounds where he could hide," said Joey.

"It's in a meadow by the river." Huck shook his head. "There's a grove of trees, and the Longhouse, and a racetrack for the rodeo. There isn't a cliff or a pile of rocks for miles."

"Clearly no place for me," declared George firmly. "I don't even want to think about it. Let's get on with today's picnic. Who wishes to Indian-wrestle first?"

"I will," offered Joan. "I'll wrestle you, George."

One after another, the stegosaurus tumbled each of them to the ground. He was proud of his easy victory and wanted to repeat the contests again, but they finally convinced him that they had to go. He accompanied them to the end of the rocky spur.

"Come back tomorrow," he urged hospitably. "We'll have another picnic, and this time I'll provide the refreshment."

"Tomorrow I promised to stack firewood," remembered Huck.

"The next day, then."

"That's the day we're going to drive in to Madras with Auntie Casey," Joan told him. "Joey wore through his tennis shoes."

"Then the day after that." George's usually mild voice took on a sharper edge.

"That's Friday. The day before the festival starts," Huck remembered. "The Longhouse is twenty miles beyond the agency. Grandfather and I will have to leave early if we expect to get there by dark."

"And we can't come the next day, because that's when we go to the festival," said Joey. "And if we don't get to go back the day after that, we'll have to help

Auntie Casey with the visitors. But maybe the day after that——"

"Please don't put yourself out on my account," said George stiffly. "We'll leave the invitation open. Come when you can."

Huck was a little uneasy about bringing the twins home with him this afternoon. Opalo had spoken of certain duties which would occupy his time, and while his grandson had no way of knowing what they were or how long they would take, he was sure that the medicine man would not welcome an interruption before they were completed. It was a relief to see the old man sitting quietly on the ground in front of the tepee.

"I have brought my friends, Grandfather," called Huck in Klickitat. "You told me they would be welcome."

Opalo bent his gray head in solemn recognition. His face was calm. Evidently the day had gone according to his calculations.

The three children came and stood before him.

"How do you do, sir?" said Joey.

"Hello," said Joan shyly, and held out the mashed parcel in waxed paper. "I brought you a present."

Opalo's brown hand reached for the cupcake. He unwrapped the paper and began to eat immediately.

"I have news, Grandfather," said Huck. "We were at the agency when the twelve scouts returned from the mountains. The berries are nearly ripe, and the festival will be in four days."

He had decided that now was not the time to mention that the scouts had driven to the mountains in a car. He might convey this information later, when the twins had gone, but he was never going to tell about Florence Bigsaw's tasting a berry before the proper time. There was no reason to outrage his grandfather's feelings, and perhaps he would never hear about it.

"We will be ready," said Opalo through a mouthful of cupcake.

"My friends would like to be present at the festival," continued Huck.

"Many whites come to our festivals these days," grunted Opalo. "They stand and stare at things they do not understand, and sometimes they laugh at moments which are most sacred. We do not try to keep them away. Our younger people welcome them."

"But my friends are not like that," insisted Huck. "They will not come except by invitation from you."

"Is this true?" Opalo looked hard first at Joey, then at Joan.

"Doesn't he want to bother with us?" whispered Joey anxiously. "Tell him we won't be any trouble. We'll do everything he says."

Suddenly Opalo smiled, and the hard stare melted into approval.

"Your friends are courteous to await an invitation," he told his grandson. "Assure them that they are welcome to attend this festival as guests of Opalo, medicine man of the Klickitats."

"He says yes," translated Huck, being especially careful how he phrased his words. "He says you'll be his guests at the festival. So you can go home and tell your Auntie Casey that everything's all right."

"Good," beamed Joey. His eyes traveled past the old

157

man to the tepee behind him. "Tell your grandfather I sure like his tepee. It's the best one I ever saw."

Huck translated rapidly, then added in English, "It's buffalo hide. My grandfather's grandfather made it."

"Could I touch it?" asked Joey respectfully. "I'll be very careful."

"Tell your friends they may go in if they like," said Opalo surprisingly. "They will be the first whites who have ever entered the tepee of our family."

The twins were delighted to accept the invitation. Huck lifted the flap and followed them in. It was close and murky, since the only light came through the opening around the center poles, but there was plenty of room, for the interior was even larger than it looked from the outside. Even after all these years, the hides gave off a faint, musky odor, and there was a smoky smell, too. Opalo must have made a fire earlier in the day, since there was a small pile of ashes in the center of the tepee.

"This is great," said Joey. "Just great. You're sure lucky, Huck, to have a swell tepee like this."

"It's my grandfather's, not mine."

"Then he's lucky."

"He's nice, too," said Joan. "He's not at all the way Mildred said." She stopped and clapped her hand over her mouth, her eyes begging Huck's pardon.

"I know," he said bitterly. "Crazy. That's what she said. It's what all the Posts say, and some of the others, too."

"That just shows how wrong they are," said Joey gruffly. "It doesn't do any good to worry about it, though. The thing to do is prove that they are wrong."

158

CHAPTER *FIFTEEN*

HUCK AND HIS GRANDFATHER were among the last to arrive at He He Longhouse, but their usual camping place was vacant. It was the same spot which Opalo had chosen long before Huck was born and which he had occupied every August, when the tribes gathered to celebrate the past harvest, and again in September, when the dwindling group of older Indians met to eat the veteran's dinner and to recall the old ways.

When he was younger, Huck had wished his grandfather had selected a location closer to the others, who always pitched their camps close together under the trees near the river. Now he was glad that they were by themselves in the open field of wild grasses, allowed to grow chest-high and bleached by the sun to the color of ripe wheat.

Old Paint had taken his usual leisurely time on the way, pausing for frequent rests. He was smart about it and always turned off onto the shoulder, pulling the wagon after him, so that cars could get by without any difficulty. Opalo didn't mind the many stops. He peered out from under his wide-brimmed hat at the occupants of the passing cars, and sometimes, when he recognized an acquaintance, he raised a hand in solemn greeting. But it was humiliating to Huck to have to sit there while everyone else speeded by in a car. Aside from the wild horses, brought in for the rodeo and the prize racers, Paint would be the only horse at the festival, certainly the only one used as a means of conveyance.

As they drew close, the smells of smoke and of roasting meat told them that supper preparations were under way. Some of the campers had built open fires before their tents, while others had been farsighted enough to bring portable barbecues from home, and the smoke was tinged with the odor of hickory and briquettes. The murmur of the river, flowing deeply in its narrow rocky bed below, was drowned out by the voices of hundreds of merrymakers come to celebrate the next three days. Dogs barked, children shouted, and from the corral behind the Longhouse a wild horse neighed in protest to captivity.

"Somebody's cooking hamburgers," said Huck wistfully. He wondered what they would have for supper. Tonight it was not a community affair. Every family provided for itself and, so far as he knew, they had brought no food with them.

"Um," grunted his grandfather, and snapped old Paint impatiently with the reins. "Get on, horse."

"Hello, there! Opalo!" called a voice from the encampment under the trees.

Paint, who had picked up a little speed in answer to his master's orders, stopped short as though he, too, realized that they were being hailed. A moment later, a burly figure in a green sport shirt and tan slacks came hurrying to intercept them. Huck recognized Burt Franchere, Lily's father; and behind him was Lily's brother, Jack.

"Charley Whitewater asked me to watch for you," Burt explained as he reached the wagon. He used the Warm Springs tongue, but the words came slowly, as though he had to stop and choose each one. "My son and I will help you set up your tepee."

"Thank you," nodded Opalo after a moment, and Huck was relieved. Opalo would not refuse the help of a friend, and he had always liked Burt Franchere. Probably that was why Chief Whitewater had selected him for this task.

Burt walked along beside the wagon, occasionally looking up to address a careful remark to Opalo, and his son followed behind. From his own high seat, Huck looked back, and Jack caught his eye and winked. Huck smiled. The wink did not imply scorn. It was only Jack's way of saying hello.

They had to hunt a long time to find the old holes, dug years before in the meadow for the tepee poles, for the grass had grown so high.

"It would be easier to dig new ones, Dad," protested Jack. "This is like looking for a needle in a haystack."

"He wants his tepee in the exact spot it's always been in." His father spoke sharply and in English. "He wouldn't be happy otherwise. It's little enough to ask. Keep looking. They're here somewhere."

"OK, OK," agreed Jack hastily, bending low to push aside the tall grass and feeling along the ground with his hands.

"I've found one," cried Huck in relief. "At least, it's a hole."

He repeated the remark in Klickitat, and his grandfather came to bend over and inspect his discovery. It was one of the old holes, he declared, although it would have to be dug out again, since winter rains had washed down loose earth.

"Your eyes are sharp, Weewino," he admitted. Then he added, as though it were a reward for the discovery, "Now you can take the horse to the corral."

With one hole as the center of operation, it was not difficult to locate the rest, and by the time Huck returned, the framework of the tepee was rising out of the tall grass.

"But you mustn't build a fire, Opalo," Burt Franchere was saying. "Charley Whitewater said you'd have to understand that. He said it was all right for you to pitch your tepee here in the old place, but he couldn't run the chance of a grass fire."

"Even a fool would know that," Opalo told him scornfully. "In the old days, the grass never grew so tall in the meadow. Your father's generation was more dutiful than yours, Burt Franchere. They came often to the Longhouse, to show respect to the Great Spirit. And after the annual burning in the fall, their many horses kept the spring growth cropped short. This meadow was like a great pasture then."

"So Vangie said to bring you and Huck back to supper," continued Burt, cheerfully ignoring the implied rebuke. "It will be ready by the time we get there."

Opalo did not answer, but Huck knew that he would accept the invitation. So far as he himself was concerned, he could hardly wait long enough to help fit the buffalo hide over the tall poles. He couldn't remember when he had been so hungry.

The encampment by the river was like a little city.

Friends had camped beside each other, and later arrivals had squeezed themselves into open spaces, so that if the original intention had been to leave connecting pathways, these had long since disappeared.

The peaked canvas spires clustered so thickly that once anyone had penetrated the outer fringe, it was impossible to see through to the wooden Longhouse, which would be the center of tomorrow's activities. Most of the tents were in the traditional tepee shape, commercially made from heavy canvas, but there were a few modern pup tents and at least one small trailer house, which had been hauled behind a car. Huck knew that there would be one tepee of buffalo hide from the Yakima Reservation, whose members were guests at the festival, but it was not nearly so large and imposing as his grandfather's. Its owner was willing to set it up in the midst of the newer counterparts, so that anyone would have to look twice to recognize it for what it was.

They walked single file, skirting tent poles and wading through family parties already eating supper. Burt led the way, followed by Opalo, then Jack and Huck. Everyone had a friendly remark for Burt Franchere, and most of them spoke to Opalo as he passed, too. But Huck noticed that while they joked with Burt for being late for supper or congratulated him because Lily had been chosen queen for this year's festival, their eyes were wary when they looked at his grandfather and their words to him were reserved. He wondered miserably what they were thinking and what they would say to each other about the old medicine man once he had gone by.

Vangie Franchere had everything ready when they arrived. She was a plump woman, in her late forties, whose black hair was still without any white, and she had a smiling, dimpled face which must have looked much like her daughter's at one time. Lily was trying to help, but she was so excited over her selection as tomorrow's queen that her mother laughingly declared she was more trouble than she was worth.

Huck was delighted to see that they were going to have hamburgers. Thick, round pats of beef were spitting over the coals of a portable barbecue, and sliced buns were warming upside down on the outer edges. On a folding card table, Vangie had set out relish and mustard, sliced tomatoes and onions, and a huge bowl of potato salad.

"Hope you like hamburgers, Huck," she said, after she had greeted Opalo courteously. "We've got lots of them."

"He likes bananas better," said Lily. "Every time he's come in the store he's asked for them."

"For Grandfather," explained Huck. "He's the one who really likes them."

"I wish I'd known." Vangie's brown eyes rested a moment on the thin figure of Opalo, slumped wearily in a metal folding chair. Tonight Opalo had been much too tired to sit on the hard ground. "You could have brought some home from the store, Lily."

"Oh, we haven't had any for days. Too hot to keep," Lily told her. "Just wait till you see my costume, Huck. It's beautiful!"

"He's seen the queen's dress before, Lily," Jack reminded her. "Everybody has. It's the same one every year."

"But never up close," insisted Lily. "From a distance, you'd never believe that buckskin could be that soft. And the beadwork! Honestly, it must have taken years to do!"

"These two are done," announced Vangie, putting buns on two plates and covering each with a thick round of smoking meat. "Give them to your father and our guest, Lily. I'll get the coffee. I set our pot to boil over Florence Bigsaw's fire."

By the time she returned with the granite coffeepot, more meat was done, and Huck was so busy eating that he hardly noticed what was going on. He was glad Mrs. Franchere had said there was plenty, and he was just beginning on his third hamburger and second helping of salad when the ringing of bells made him look up from his plate.

At that moment an errant breeze, which had worked its way through the canvas maze of tepees, filled his eyes with charcoal smoke from the barbecue, so that he could not see. But, above the ringing of bells, he could hear a high-pitched voice.

"Hocus-pocus mumbo jumbo. Come out, Monster! Show yourself!"

There was a familiar ring to that voice, which broke into a little giggle at the word "monster," and Huck hurried to wipe back the tears which the smoke had called forth. Standing on the other side of the barbecue were two figures, and despite the fact that they were wearing other than their customary clothing, Huck recognized them instantly.

165

Nappy Post had on a sleeveless leather vest, and his bare arms were encircled with bright-colored strips of tin, which looked suspiciously like the unwinding bands of metal cans. About his neck were several long strings, from which dangled an assortment of bones, fresh from some butcher shop. His head was covered by a wig made of unraveled rope, and protruding from the wig were two old cow horns, with a sleigh bell dangling from each tip. His face was daubed with streaks and circles of red and blue paint.

Bob Catchum was the monster, and he threw off an old dark blanket when he heard himself being summoned. The rest of his costume consisted of a home-made, hideously painted paper mask and swim fins, which he wore on his hands. These flapped around in a manner which threatened to upset the barbecue.

"What's all this?" demanded Burt Franchere. His voice sounded as though he didn't know whether to laugh or be angry.

"It's just us, Mr. Franchere," said Nappy quickly, and Bob let the swim fins drop to his side. "We didn't have anything to wear in tomorrow's parade, so we fixed these up ourselves. How d'you like them? I'm a medicine man, and Bob's the monster I put under my spell. My folks think it's a panic."

"Do they?" said Burt uneasily. Huck saw him glance at Opalo.

"They are still small children and play the games of children," said Opalo disapprovingly. "When I was their age, I was a man. But perhaps those two will never be men."

"Oh, they'll grow up sometime. They don't really

167

mean anything," Burt told him uncomfortably. Then, speaking in English, he said, "You run along now, kids. I don't think it's as funny as your folks do. Some of our older people take these things pretty seriously."

"Sure, Mr. Franchere," giggled Nappy, and, with a jangling of sleigh bells, he and Bob disappeared behind the next tepee.

"I hate them," declared Huck bitterly. "They dressed that way to bring shame to my grandfather and to me."

"Oh no, Huck." Mrs. Franchere leaned forward and patted his knee comfortingly. "I don't think they meant that at all. Everyone will be dressed up tomorrow, and they just wanted to be specially fancy."

"No, they didn't," he insisted stubbornly. "And my grandfather's never going to go live with the Posts, no matter what Chief Whitewater says. We'll run away first, both of us. Far away, where they can't find us."

"Live with the Posts?" repeated Burt in amazement. "What do you mean, Huck?"

But Huck didn't wait to answer. He had to get away, to be by himself. No one would stop Nappy and Bob from enacting their little scene tomorrow. Some people would think it was amusing, others would call it childish play. But Huck was sure that it was a deliberate intent to be cruel, to make everyone laugh at a man they had once held in respect.

He walked along the riverbank, away from the encampment, and when he found a log, he sat down and listened to the night voices of the stream, so very different from those of the daytime. It was dark by now. A million stars glittered overhead, but they were not the friendly stars they had always seemed to be at home. Tonight they looked cold, and far away, and critical.

He had gone too far to hear the sounds from the camp, but he knew that they were there. People would be talking and laughing, perhaps at Nappy and Bob as they passed from fire to fire, playing the medicine man and the monster. It was all Huck's fault, too. If he hadn't called them to the spring that day, expecting to produce a monster, they would never have had such an idea.

It was very late when he finally decided to return. Even the most determined celebrators would be in bed by this time, for the festival would begin early the next morning. As he stepped out onto the road which ran beside the river, Huck stopped. He could see no one, yet a hidden sense seemed to tell him that he was not alone. He dropped to his knees and put his ear to the graveled surface. His grandfather had told him that it was in this way that the ancient ones learned of approaching horsemen; they could feel reverberation of the pounding hoofs. Huck had never tried it before, but to his surprise he could hear, or thought he heard, the thump-thump-thump of someone approaching around the curve. He darted back to hide among the shadows.

For a moment, the narrow road lay bare in the moonlight; then suddenly it was choked with rocks. They filled it from side to side, and although the ground was level, the rocks appeared to be slipping forward with the sureness of lava running down a mountainside. Huck gulped, then stepped forward.

"George!" he called.

The rocks quivered and shook in the moonlight; then they stood still.

"Huck!" cried the stegosaurus happily. "I knew I would find you. My instinct told me so. But I didn't get your scent before you spoke. Perhaps the wind is blowing the other way."

"What are you doing here?" demanded Huck in amazement. "I thought you were afraid of all the people."

"I am." George shivered, and his spiked tail pounded against the roadbed. "But you are my friend, and I trust you to hide me from them. Everyone else is going to the picnic, and I want to go, too. I want to watch the Indian wrestling, so make sure the hiding place you choose will give me a good view of that."

"But I can't hide you," objected Huck. "There's no place here to hide."

"Poor, poor mammal," clucked George sympathetically. "Poor little tiny-brained mammal! Don't you remember that your movable cave serves me just as well as rimrock? You will hide me inside of that, naturally."

CHAPTER *SIXTEEN*

"HURRY UP," urged Joey for the tenth time in the last hour. "We've got to get started. We might miss something."

"You could have helped with the dishes," Joan reminded him reproachfully. "I'd have finished with them faster."

"It wasn't my turn. I did them yesterday," Joey told her reasonably. "I wonder how many bananas there are here, anyway."

"Seventeen," said Joan crossly, rinsing her dishcloth under the tap and squeezing it out. "You counted them twice since we got home and once at the store."

"We could have made a mistake. They're hard to count when they overlap like this." Joey frowned. He held up the long stalk and began counting the bananas at the bottom.

He and Joan were both proud of this present they were taking to Huck's grandfather. The store where they had shopped in Madras sold bananas. Generally, they were broken off and piled on a counter, but these had been left on a long stalk which was suspended from a beam. The fruit had been cut from the top to fill individual orders, and only a dozen or so golden bananas clung tightly to what looked like a stiff length of brown rope. Auntie Casey had intended that the clerk break off a few and put them in a paper bag, but Joey had stopped her in time.

"Why don't we buy the whole thing? I bet Huck's grandfather would like it better."

"Whatever for?" demanded Auntie Casey in amazement. "Nobody buys banana stalks. We'll just take a dollar's worth."

Joan and Joey exchanged quick glances as they shared an idea.

"How many bananas do you get for a dollar?" Joey asked the clerk.

"Oh, I don't know," he said good-naturedly. "These aren't too large. I'd say they'd run about five bananas to a pound and a half."

Joan began counting the fruit, holding one hand on the spot where she began, to mark her place.

"What are you doing?" asked Auntie Casey in amazement.

"She's going to see how many bananas there are," explained Joey. "If they're nineteen cents a pound and five of them make a pound and a half, you wouldn't have to break them off to see how much they came to, would you?"

"No, I guess not." The clerk grinned at Auntie Casey, who was shaking her head in astonishment. "If the kids want the stem, they can sure have it. We'll just throw it away."

Joan's count came out seventeen bananas, and the clerk obligingly figured it out for them. It came to ninety-five cents—and since Auntie Casey had been prepared to spend a whole dollar, the twins were quick to point out that they had saved her money.

They both sat in the back seat on the drive home, holding the stem between them, so that the bananas would not get mashed. When they arrived, the stalk was hung on a nail over the kitchen door. This meant that anyone going into the living room had to duck under, but it was pleasant to see it hanging there and to anticipate the pleasure of Huck's grandfather on receiving this extraordinary gift.

"They're getting awfully soft," worried Joey as he finished his recount of the fruit. "It's a good thing we give them to him today."

"They ought to be kept where it's cool." Joan frowned. "Maybe when we drive to the festival we could put them in the trunk. You know how hot it is in the car."

"The trunk's even hotter."

"It wouldn't be if we took ice," she reminded him. "If we had a bucket of ice in the trunk, the bananas would keep nice and cool."

"You get the ice cubes," agreed Joey, wondering why he hadn't thought of the idea himself. "I'll find something to put them in."

Mildred's scrub bucket served very nicely, and although the cubes from four ice trays made only a little mound in the bottom, Joey and Joan decided it was enough to cool the temperature. The stiff stalk was fitted in at an angle, with the bananas next to the galvanized bucket. Auntie Casey came hurrying from the house just as Joey slammed down the trunk lid.

"Are you children ready? I've got to get back before people start coming. The weatherman says it's going to be a scorcher in town, so we'll probably have a crowd."

As they bumped along over the gravel road, she gave them last-minute instructions.

"Now you're not to swim in the river. There's too much current there, and it's too deep. And when the rodeo's on, sit well back, just in case one of those wild animals jumps the fence. And if you're in any kind of trouble, or if anything happens, find Mildred——"

"Or Huck's grandfather," interposed Joey.

"Yes," she agreed a little grudgingly. "But since I don't know him, or how close an eye he keeps on youngsters, I'm counting more on Mildred. I didn't even mention to her that you'd asked Huck's grandfather to keep an eye on you, too. Sometimes she takes offense at little things that seem unimportant to us. But she understands exactly what you can do and what you can't, because I told her."

"Yes, Auntie Casey," said Joan quickly, giving Joey a "don't argue" look.

Although it was early when they arrived, the field which had been designated as a parking lot was already crowded with cars. Many of them belonged to the Indians who were camped in the grove, but additional visitors were arriving, and on the road in from the agency they had found themselves in a steady stream of automobiles.

"How in the world are we going to find Mildred in all this crowd?" worried Auntie Casey.

"There's Huck!" cried Joey in excitement. "Standing there by the road. Stop, Auntie Casey! Stop!"

"Gracious me!" Auntie Casey thrust her arm from

the car window, waving it up and down as a signal to the car behind her.

"Come on, Joan," screamed Joey, fumbling with the door handle.

"Are you sure it's Huck?" Aunt Casey squinted through the dust at the small figure standing beside the field of parked cars. He was dressed for the festival in a fringed leather bib and a short leather skirt, which was open on each side to show thin, brown legs to his waist. About his head was a fold of scarlet cloth, into which had been thrust a stiff brown feather.

Both children were out of the car by this time and had run around to join the leather-clad figure by the road. Cars in the long procession began to toot their horns, impatient of the delay. Auntie Casey took her foot from the brake and reluctantly began to move along.

"Find Mildred," she shouted. "I'll meet you here at seven-thirty. Be good."

"We will," cried Joan dutifully as the car rolled on around the field, where it could rejoin the road back to the agency.

"You sure look keen, Huck," said Joey admiringly. "That's a real Indian costume, isn't it? Not one of those things made out of old brown cloth that you buy in the store."

Huck nodded his head shyly.

"And your moccasins are beautiful. All those tiny little beads!" marveled Joan.

"They were my mother's," admitted Huck. "She did the embroidery before she died. I cannot wear them much longer, for my feet are getting too big."

"Have we missed anything?" demanded Joey. "Has it started?"

"No." Huck shook his head. Then his face grew worried. "But there is something I must tell you. We——"

Joey clapped his hand to his cheek and stared at his sister accusingly.

"The bananas! You left the bananas in the car!"

"Maybe we can catch Auntie Casey," cried Joan. "Maybe she hasn't had time to get back to the road yet!"

The twins started across the field, threading their way through cars which were parked in irregular lines, and Huck ran after them. The ground was rough and hilly, so it was impossible to make very good time. They arrived at the intersection of the road just behind Auntie Casey's sedan as it lurched onto the graveled surface and picked up speed. Their calls must have been drowned by the sound of the motor, and since she did not turn her head, she did not see them.

"What was it?" asked Huck. "Did you change your mind about staying at the festival?"

"Oh, we want to stay, all right," Joey assured him. "Only we brought a present for your grandfather and forgot and left it in the car."

"Bananas," explained Joan. "Still growing on the stem. I hope they don't spoil before Auntie Casey gets back this evening. She didn't know we put them in the trunk."

"That was very kind of you," said Huck gratefully. "He will be pleased. But I must tell you something important. George is here."

"George!" repeated Joey, forgetting about the bananas in his amazement. "Our George?"

"He came last night." Huck nodded. "Very late. No one saw him, because it was dark. And he expects us to keep him hidden so he can watch the Indian wrestling."

"Where is he now?" gasped Joan.

"He's in our tepee. Or at least as much of him as he can get in. There isn't room for his tail. That sticks out behind, but the grass is pretty high. All that really shows are the tops of the spikes, and I don't think anybody's going to notice them. They're pointed away from the Longhouse, and nobody goes into that field."

"Well, then, he's perfectly safe," declared Joey. "And I'm glad he decided to come. It's probably very lonely being the only stegosaurus in the whole world."

"You don't understand," said Huck hopelessly. "My grandfather might get tired and go back to the tepee. He got up early this morning, long before daylight. That's how I could get George inside before anyone saw him. He just waited around in the field until my grandfather left. Now he's inside, looking out a little crack, and he says we're his friends and we invited him to the festival, so it's up to us to keep everybody away until dark."

"Isn't there some other place your grandfather could go to rest?" asked Joan.

"I suppose so. But he won't."

"We'd better tell him about George, I guess. Sort of prepare him," decided Joey.

"We can't," Joan reminded him quickly. "Don't you

remember? A long time ago we promised not to ever talk about him to outsiders."

"That was at home, on Cricket Creek."

"It's still a promise, no matter where we are."

"And I promised never to bring strangers to see him, after the time I brought Nappy and Bob," recalled Huck. "Of course, I wouldn't be bringing my grandfather, and it is his tepee, but George wouldn't understand that. He expects me to keep people away."

"Maybe we'd better talk to him," decided Joey. "Where is he, Huck?"

Huck hurried them along the road beside the parked cars. The tepee city lay on their right, a fascinating labyrinth of canvas spires, which the twins would have liked to explore, and the Longhouse lay straight ahead, a little to their left.

At first glance, the Longhouse presented a bleak and dull appearance, for it was nothing but a long building, built of unpainted wood, with a conventional roof which hung over the front to form a sort of porch. But the area directly in front made up for any lack of color. Here were the concessions to be found in any fair— a hot-dog stand, another which manufactured and sold fluffy pink cotton candy, dart games with shelves of gaily dressed dolls and stuffed animals to be won as prizes, a shooting gallery, an ice-cream vendor, a popcorn wagon. Despite the early hour, all were doing a brisk business. They were operated by smiling, shouting, brown-skinned Indians, who wore comfortable American sport shirts and, in honor of the occasion, feathers in their hair.

"Let's get a hot dog," suggested Joey, hesitating as they passed. "I'm hungry."

"It takes too long." Joan tried to push him ahead. "We've got to see George and tell him we can't be responsible for what happens."

"Some popcorn, then," compromised Joey. "You don't have to wait for that to cook."

He dashed over to the popcorn wagon and a moment later rejoined them with a tall bag filled with fragrant, salted corn, which he passed around.

As they walked down the side of the gray building, the twins were surprised at its length. The Longhouse was truly named. It was much larger than it appeared from the front and would hold many people. Straight ahead, they could see Opalo's tepee rising out of the waving field of tall grass.

"It looks a little bulgy," observed Joey critically. "George makes it stick out in places. I hope nobody notices."

"I think they're all too busy," said Joan. "But I wish he hadn't come. I don't like to feel responsible. Maybe they'll have the Indian wrestling early and he can leave."

"He can't leave till it gets dark," Joey reminded her.

George was delighted to see them. His remarks were muffled by the thick buffalo hide, for he was much too nervous to poke his whole head outside. Somehow he had managed to drape two sides of the opening flap across his nose, so that one eye could peer through the small slit.

"I'm glad you are here," he told them. "All these smells of unfamiliar mammals are very distressing. I've

never been so close to so many before. You shouldn't have coaxed me to come."

"We didn't coax you to come," said Joey. "We just said we wished you could."

"It's the same thing," insisted George. "I wouldn't have even known about picnics if it hadn't been for you. When will it start?"

"Pretty soon," Huck assured him. "The parade will be first. Maybe you could get away while everyone's looking at that. The only thing you'd have to be careful about then would be the highway. Some of the visitors come late."

"Now that I'm here, I shall certainly stay for the picnic," declared the stegosaurus. "So far I haven't had a bite to eat, and there's been no Indian wrestling at all."

"Have some popcorn," offered Joey hastily, thrusting the sack into the slit between the buffalo hides.

"Thank you," said George, amid the noises of crunching kernels and rustling paper. "Is that all there is? I knew there wouldn't be enough food."

"It's all for now," Joey told him. "We'll get you something more later on. The thing is, George, Huck's grandfather will be coming here to rest pretty soon. When he does, he'll find you."

"Gracious!" exclaimed George in alarm, and they could hear a series of hard, dull thumps as his tail bit into the dry earth behind the tepee. "Are you sure he's coming here?"

"Not until afternoon," said Huck. "He'll stay for the dances and for the feast. But in the afternoon, when they have the rodeo and the races, he's pretty sure to come here to rest for a while."

"Thank you for warning me." The tepee trembled with George's shudder. "I shall be gone by then. I certainly won't be here when he comes."

"While they're having the parade is the best time to get away," Huck told him. "And don't feel too bad about missing the Indian wrestling. They'll have it over in the center of the racetrack, so you couldn't have seen it from here anyway."

"And where is the racetrack?" asked George in surprise.

"Over by the horse corrals. You can't see it from here. The grandstand's in the way."

"Thank you for telling me," said George gratefully. "You see, this is so new. I've never tried to attend a picnic like this before."

"We'll have our own next week," Joan promised him. "We'll come to your cave to have it. And we'll bring all the things you like best to eat. And we'll Indian-wrestle and Indian-wrestle."

CHAPTER *SEVENTEEN*

"WE REALLY OUGHT
to take George something more to eat before he leaves,"
said Joey as they walked back to the festival grounds.

"We can't take a hot dog, because he's a vegetarian,"
remembered Joan. "But I'll bet he'd like some cotton
candy. Poor thing. Coming all this way for nothing."

But by the time they reached the Longhouse, there
was no time to buy a treat for the stegosaurus. The
parade was forming, and Huck had to find his place in
the procession.

"You'd better get up in front where you can see,"
he advised before he left. "I'll find you again as soon
as it's over."

Many more visitors had arrived while they were in
the field talking with George, for the Huckleberry Festival had been publicized in the city papers and crowds
had driven out to witness the event. Spectators were
jammed three- and four-deep along both sides of the
road. Joey and Joan took Huck's advice and squeezed
themselves through to the front row, but they were a
little annoyed to find that they were standing next to
Mildred Post.

"Hi," she greeted them cheerfully. "I been looking
for you. I told your aunt I'd keep my eye on you."

"Shouldn't you be in the parade, Mildred?" asked
Joey.

"Oh, I been in enough of them in my time." She laughed. "I thought this year I'd just watch. You don't have to march, you know, though they like it if you do. But most of my family's going to be in it, so I thought they could do without me. Well, what do you think of it? Having a good time?"

"It's very nice," said Joan.

"But it would be better if everybody wore real costumes. Like Huck's," said Joey frankly.

Although he had observed that almost every Indian present was wearing soft moccasins, that was the only universal concession made to native dress. Each wore what he pleased, and the result was a heterogeneous mixture of modern clothing, with only touches of Indian trappings in honor of the occasion. Some of the women wore gay shawls and velvet-trimmed gowns; others wore modern pedal pushers, with many shell and bead necklaces over their cotton blouses. Outside of the tribal costumes worn by the paraders, the men were dressed in soft, cotton shirts, with beaded belts above their modern slacks and with here and there a feathered headdress.

"If it's costumes you want, wait till you see my nephew Nappy's getup," chuckled Mildred. "He's rigged himself up like an old-time medicine man. His best friend, Bob Catchum, is supposed to be the ogreish thing the medicine man conjures up. They put on a real show, them two. I laughed till I hurt. And to think that only a few years ago people actually believed in that stuff."

"Huck's grandfather's a medicine man," said Joan.

"And time was when folks used to actually believe he

could drive out evil spirits, too." She chuckled. "Well, the parade's starting. There go the drums. About time, too. My feet are killing me already from standing around so long."

Once it was under way, even Joey had to admit that he was glad they were watching the parade with Mildred, for she was able to explain things they would never have understood. First came twelve women in tribal dress, with woven carrying baskets on their backs. These were the scouts who had been to the mountains for huckleberries and who would serve as hostesses for the feast. One of them was so old that she had to be helped along by two others, but most of them were much younger.

Then came the chief of the federated tribes in a beaded, fringed costume with a huge war bonnet, and after him walked Huck's grandfather. His face was so hidden with streaks of paint that the twins would not have recognized him if Mildred hadn't told them who he was. He wore a sleeveless leather jacket, from which his bony arms protruded like thin brown sticks. Each arm was loaded with metal and leather bracelets, from which dangled various objects that Martha told them had once had tribal significance, although no one re-membered what it was anymore. Opalo's short, fringed skirt was much like the one Huck had worn, and more charms clanked about each ankle. On his head was a wig made of long black horsehair, which kept blowing across his painted face so that it was a wonder he could see at all. Protruding from the horsehair were forked antlers.

"Would you believe that people used to be scared

of him?" asked Mildred in a loud voice, which made the twins squirm uncomfortably. "When he said something, they used to jump."

To their relief, Opalo did not glance in their direction. He continued to march on, looking straight ahead, the charms on his arms and ankles clanging and rattling and the assorted objects, which hung from buckskin strands about his neck, bobbing up and down with each step.

"The queen'll be next," confided Mildred. "This year it's Lily Franchere. But there'll be a little wait, because the court's on horseback and Old Martha, one of the berry scouts, has to take it so slow."

At last the royal court came riding by, and the twins were beside themselves with pride because they were personally acquainted with the queen. Her fringed doeskin dress was almost as white as the horse she rode. It was heavy with beads, and the design was matched by the beaded trappings of her mount. With every step, tiny bells pealed out a silver salute to her subjects.

Behind her princesses followed the other marchers. First came the older braves, then the pre-teen boys, who would soon be admitted to the braves' standing. Huck was in this group, and he looked over and smiled shyly at the twins as he passed by. Finally came the women and smaller children.

"Where's your nephew?" asked Joey pointedly. Both twins had looked for Nappy and Bob in the group of pre-teen boys and had been surprised when they weren't there.

"He'll be last. Before the horses," chuckled Mildred. "He plans to stop as he goes along and put on his little act. Chief Whitewater said he couldn't do that and hold up the marchers. He says it's kid stuff, and maybe it is, but it's sure funny. You can hear people laughing back there now."

Something very funny was happening down the line, for the spectators were giggling and guffawing loudly. The thick crowd kept the twins from seeing what was going on, but before long two figures dashed into view to take up a stand in the road only a few feet away. One was completely shrouded in a dark blanket, but the second wore a wig with horns, a sleeveless vest, and metal strips around his arms.

"That's him." Mildred nudged them with her elbow. "That's Nappy."

"Why, he's dressed up to look like Huck's grandfather," gasped Joan.

"That's what I told you," nodded Mildred. "He's supposed to be a medicine man calling up an evil spirit. Now watch."

For thirty seconds or so, Nappy executed a little dance in the dusty road. His body bent nearly double, and he lifted his feet high as he circled round and round, chanting, "Wa, wa. Wa, wa, wa." Then he straightened up, lifted his arms, and shouted, "Hocus-pocus mumbo jumbo. Come out, evil spirit!"

The dark blanket was thrown back and from behind a painted mask, the monster screamed.

"Boo!"

Amid the laughter of the spectators, the medicine man and the monster bowed deeply. Then the dark blanket was thrown over the monster's head, and the two trotted on to repeat the performance farther down the line.

"I think that's perfectly awful!" cried Joan indignantly.

"Awful?" Mildred stopped laughing to stare at her in amazement.

"To make fun of Huck's grandfather that way."

"Oh, him," scoffed Mildred. "He don't know what's going on."

"He does, too," insisted Joey. "And he's our friend. And we're going to go find him right now. Come on, Joan."

"But I'm supposed to keep an eye on you," she protested. "And, anyway, the parade's not over. There'll still be the horses and riders."

"We don't want to see the horses," said Joan over her shoulder. "And don't worry about us, Mildred. We're perfectly all right."

Since the parade route was so short, those who had started were beginning to disband even before the horsemen started. The twelve berry scouts had already gone inside the Longhouse, and Chief Whitewater and Opalo were standing side by side on the steps. Joey, with Joan only a few steps behind, advanced straight to the old medicine man.

"Good morning, sir," he said loudly, as though a firm tone would make up for a language barrier. "You remember me? I'm Joey Brown, and this is my sister, Joan. We're Huck's friends."

"He doesn't speak English, son," said Chief Whitewater, smiling down at them.

"Well, would you tell him, please, that we're glad to

be here? And that our aunt is proud that a medicine man is going to look after us. And that there's a present for him in her car that we'll give him this evening when she comes for us."

"I'm afraid I can't tell him all that." Chief Whitewater shook his head ruefully. "I only speak a word or two of his language myself."

Opalo had given no previous indication that he knew they were there. He had been staring straight ahead over the heads of the crowd. Now he seemed to come to with a start, as though someone had tapped him on the shoulder. The proud, stiff neck bent so that he was looking at the twins, and while Chief Whitewater stared in open amazement, the stern face cracked into a smile.

"Welcome," said Opalo distinctly and in English. He looked at them each in turn and repeated the word: "Welcome."

"I never heard him do that before," marveled the chief. "I didn't know he knew even one word of English."

"I bet he can do a lot of things you don't know about," said Joey stoutly. "You have to be pretty smart to be a medicine man."

"I guess you do." The chief smiled pleasantly.

When Huck was able to join them, they tried to watch the end of the parade, but by this time the crowd was so dense that they were unable to get through.

"I wonder if George got away without being seen," worried Joan. "Shall we go look?"

"We can tell by the shape of the tepee," remembered Joey. "We don't have to go clear out there. If it doesn't bulge anymore, he's gone."

They plowed their way through the mob to the end of the Longhouse, where they had an unrestricted view of the field. Only an expanse of tall, waving grasses greeted them.

"He's gone, all right," declared Joey.

"But he knocked over the tepee getting out," sighed Huck. "It's flat to the ground. I'll have to go put it up again."

"I'll help you," promised Joey. "But at least he got away. I was really worried. Shall we go put it up now?"

"We'll have time after the feast," decided Huck. "Grandfather won't want to rest before then. They'll be starting the dances pretty soon. If we go there now, we can get a good place to watch."

"We said hello to your grandfather," confided Joan as they walked along the edge of the crowd still watching the riders in the parade. "He said we were welcome."

"Did he?" Huck smiled widely.

"And we talked to the chief," Joey told him. "How come he can't talk Indian?"

Huck looked down at his moccasins, their beaded embroidery now dulled by the dust.

"He is young," he admitted. "The youngest chief we ever had. But he is smart. They say he is the smartest chief since the great Sim-tus-tus. He has been to college, where he learned many things that are useful. He learned so much that he forgot some of the things he knew before, such as how to speak the tongue of his fathers. He does not think that is important, and there are enough who agree with him, so that Warm Springs is seldom spoken. But Chief Whitewater has done much good for the tribes, and it is well to have a chief who works so hard. Still, there are many who say he should not have been chosen, that it would have been better to chose a chief who stays closer to the old ways and is not always thinking of progress. There are many who speak the old tongue who might have made good chiefs, but they were not chosen. They are not leaders, and under them we would not advance so far."

"He didn't look very advanced today," remembered Joey. "He looked like a real, sure-enough Indian chief."

"He is," said Huck quickly. "He does honor to his chieftain robes. And he will keep the old ways so far as he can, but when they stand in the way of progress, he will let them go."

The dancers were assembling, and a crowd was already beginning to collect around a rough square marked off on one side of the Longhouse. Generations of stomping feet had discouraged the grass, so that only a few hardy tufts had managed to survive, and the packed brown earth would soon be loosened into dust.

At one side of the square squatted the drummers, who would beat out the rhythms of the ceremonial dancers, and close beside them were the singers, whose voices would chant the meaningful words. The dancers were gathering behind the musicians, awaiting their turns, and the twins were especially impressed by one of them, who, Huck told them, would interpret the Hobo Eagle. He wore a gray-feathered headdress with a yellow bill, and when he lowered his head, the face of a bird regarded the spectators through shining glass eyes. Elaborate feathered wings were fastened from his shoulders to his fingertips, so that he could dip and soar, simulating the flight of the real bird.

There was also a dancer wearing an animal mask, who would star in the cougar dance, and loin-clothed hunters, armed with bows and arrows, to bring him down. Huck told them there would also be a snake dance, a scalp dance, the proposal dance, the moon-

light dance, and many others. Each had its special significance, and it would take some time to enact them all.

"When will they start?" asked Joey impatiently.

"Pretty soon," promised Huck. "They have to wait till all the dancers are here, and some of them rode horses in the parade."

He broke off speaking to smile at a burly warrior in a feathered war bonnet who was deliberately crossing the empty square and heading straight for them. There were streaks of blue paint down each cheek, and another streak on his forehead, but they did not hide the reproachful look on his brown face.

"Hello, Mr. Franchere," called Huck eagerly. "I want you to meet my friends, Joey and Joan Brown."

"Hello, kids." The feathered bonnet bobbed at them each in turn; then the warrior returned his attention to Huck. "Why didn't you tell me your grandfather wanted to move his tepee? Jack and I would have helped. It's too heavy for the two of you to lift."

"The tepee?" repeated Huck. "Oh, it just fell down, Mr. Franchere. Joey and I are going to fix it after the feast."

"What are you talking about?" The painted face grew stern. "Your grandfather's tepee's not down. It's up. And it's not where we put it last night. It's clear across on the other side of the field, close to the racetrack. Do you mean you didn't help your grandfather move it there?"

Huck shook his head.

"Well, maybe somebody else gave him a hand," decided Mr. Franchere after a moment. "But whoever it was didn't know much about setting up a tepee. It looks like they've broken some of the poles. It sticks out like a porcupine. If I'd had any idea that Opalo wanted it somewhere else—but he's always set it up in that spot before."

"I better go see," said Huck in a choked voice.

"We'll go with you," declared Joey quickly. "Come on."

CHAPTER *EIGHTEEN*

"I HAD TO MOVE." George's voice, coming through the tiny slit between the folds of buffalo hide, was impatient at their lack of understanding. "You said so yourself. Someone was planning to come there. Besides, I could not see the Indian wrestling from there."

"But now Grandfather will come here. He'll come to the tepee," insisted Huck.

"I wish that you would make up your mind. First you said he was coming *there*. So I left *there* and came *here*. Now he may go *there*, for I am somewhere else," explained George. "The idea was entirely logical, since this is a movable cave. I just started walking, and it moved along with me."

"Huck's grandfather will go wherever the tepee is, George," Joan told him sadly. "And when he does, he'll find you. There isn't very much we can do about it, unless you leave while people are eating."

"But I haven't had any picnic," he protested. "And that's what I came for."

"If you don't care whether people see you," said Joey. "If you want to stay here and be looked at, we can't stop you."

"Of course I care!" The tall grass rustled with the twitching of the stegosaurus's tail. "You knew how shy I was when you invited me. Now that I've yielded to my instinct and come, I expect you to protect me. That can't be so very hard to do. I'm completely concealed by this movable cave. It's very like my own cliffs. I can see out, but no one can see me. All I expect of you is to keep people away."

"It's not quite the same," objected Joey, eyeing the altered shape of the buffalo hide. He could quite understand how Mr. Franchere believed the supporting poles had been bent or broken. The straight, taut lines were gone, and the old skins were strained to cover the bony shields surrounding the reptile's spine. It was a good thing that George was standing in tall grass, for there was not enough hide to cover him entirely. It stopped a little above the great padded feet. "Besides," he added, "your tail sticks out behind."

"Then tuck it in," ordered the stegosaurus.

Although they tried, the great tail was not meant to be curled like a cat's. It continued to extend stiffly behind, the four sharp spikes protruding above the grass tops.

"Maybe we could pile some boards up against them," said Joey. "People might look at the boards and not stop to wonder what was holding them up."

"When I took Paint down to the corral, I saw a couple of old rotten fence rails," remembered Huck. "Somebody had put in new ones and left the old ones lying there. They're sort of dingy gray, too, just about like George."

The discarded fence rails proved to be just the thing. The wood was so old that it almost fell apart in their hands, and they were able to break it into the proper lengths. Piled in conical fashion about the sharp spikes, the boards made a fair camouflage, at least from a distance.

"Of course, if you come up close, you can see that it's more than a lot of old boards," admitted Joey. "But I don't think anybody'll be wading through all this grass. It's got stickeries in it."

"Except my grandfather," Huck reminded him sadly.

"Maybe he won't want to rest after all," said Joan hopefully. "Not till it gets dark. And then George will be willing to leave."

"I'll go as soon as I've enjoyed all the picnic," agreed the stegosaurus. "And I'm really getting impatient for things to begin."

"We'd better find something for him to eat," declared Joan hastily.

Huck glanced over his shoulders. The crowd was beginning to disperse, which meant that the ceremonial dances were at an end. It had taken longer than any of them had realized to arrange the boards around George's tail.

"They'll be starting the feast now," Huck said. "We'll bring something back from there."

The twelve women who had headed the morning's parade stood under the overhanging roof of the Long-house, welcoming the guests. The carrying baskets strapped on their backs were now filled with small blue huckleberries, and the air was sweet with their aroma. As the children stepped up onto the porch, the oldest of the women caught sight of Huck and called him to her with a wave of her thin, brown hand. She spoke rapidly, and in a tongue which the twins could not understand, but they had the uncomfortable feeling that some of the talk concerned them, for her face turned once in their direction. Her tone was scolding, and the old face was unsmiling, but they could not see her eyes, for they were sunk so deeply in the flesh.

Huck answered her in the same language, and first he seemed to be apologizing for something; then, when the old woman glanced at his friends, he looked at them, too, and smiled. After that, he motioned that they were to follow, and the three walked past the old woman and into the Longhouse.

The interior was even more rustic than it had appeared from without, but it had a festive appearance. The roof beams had been hung with pine and fir boughs. Their spicy fragrance rushed up to greet arrivals, and the smell reminded the twins of Christmas morning. At the far end of the room sat the chief, whose bright, feathered headdress and glittering bead embroidery made a vivid splotch of color against the rough board walls. Beside him sat his musicians, the drums already beating out the ancient rhythm by which the tribes said thank you to the harvest gods. Next to the musicians came the elders in the tribes, the old ones in whose memories still lived a recollection of a time when this festival had more meaning. They, like the chief, wore the full regalia of their fathers, but their numbers were pitifully few.

On either side of the room, stretched from wall to wall, were strips of checkered tablecloth. The red and white squares were laid on the ground, directly in front of long benches built against the walls. As people

entered the door, they turned either to left or right and filled in the seats as they came.

"I'll go first," said Huck softly. "Stay right behind me."

Joey and Joan did as they were told, and it was not until they were seated between their friend and the members of an Indian family, who had followed closely on their heels, that they realized they were among the few white persons in the room.

"Are you sure it's all right for us to be here?" worried Joan, leaning past her brother to speak to Huck.

"Oh yes. That's what Martha told me when we came in. My grandfather said you were his guests."

"She didn't look very happy about it," remembered

Joey. "She looked like she was bawling you out for something."

"Not for your being here," Huck assured him quickly. "Martha would not question my grandfather's guests. It was for something else. Something I did not do—a message I did not give to my grandfather. I didn't want to upset him."

The benches were almost filled by this time. People were squeezed so tightly together that Joey wondered how they would be able to eat. Perhaps, when the food was served, some of them would sit on the ground. If that was so, he hoped he could be one who did. It was a long way down to the checkered tablecloth.

The drumming grew louder, and the singers at the end of the room began a chant.

"Wa, wa, wa, wa, wa," they sang. There were no real words, and the melody consisted of only a few notes repeated again and again. Before long the people on the benches began to sing, too, clapping their hands with the drumbeats.

"Could we, too?" Joey whispered, and when Huck nodded, he began to sing and clap along with the others. The many voices rolled and echoed against the rafters, and the clapping hands sounded like an army of marching horses all stepping in perfect time.

Presently, three of the twelve women appeared in the doorway. They held great platters containing steaming baked salmon. They carried them to the center of the room and placed them carefully on the ground.

"Mesoch," called one of the women, and Chief White-water rose gravely to his feet and, in an echoing voice, repeated, "Mesoch."

"I thought you said he couldn't speak Indian," whispered Joey accusingly.

"A few words," frowned Huck. "Everybody knows that *mesoch* means salmon."

Three more women now entered with baskets, which they proclaimed, before setting them on the ground, to contain *piachee,* or herbs. They were followed by three more, who placed their baskets of *weewinos* next to the herbs. Finally the last three hostesses carried in jugs of clear water.

One of the old men beside the chief now arose and began speaking in his native tongue.

"He's saying thanks to the Great Spirit for the harvest and for all this food," whispered Huck.

"It doesn't look like much food. Not for all these people," said Joey frankly.

"This is just one bite for everybody," explained Huck. "It's got to be eaten the way they brought it in—first the salmon, then the herbs, then the berries, and then a sip of water. After that, they'll bring lots of everything. You'll see."

When the elder had finished speaking, the hostesses began serving. As Huck had said, this was a single bite of everything for everyone there. Later on, there would be plates and cups and silverware put down on the tablecloth, but for one bite the twins could see that such utensils were hardly necessary. This was much like the appetizers sometimes served before dinner.

By the time everyone had been served, the containers in the center were empty, and the hostesses gathered them up and hurried away. The tribesmen had been comparatively quiet while the ceremony had been going on, but now conversations began to break out. They remembered that it was a festival. People had come to enjoy themselves.

Then suddenly, on each side of the great room, people began saying "Sh" to one another. Necks craned toward the end occupied by the chief and the elders, and everything grew quiet once more as they realized that the old medicine man of the Klickitats was on his feet and making a speech.

Opalo's voice was firm. It did not quaver with age but rang out deeply, angrily. He spoke in his own tongue, so that more than half of those present could not understand everything he said, but there was something impelling in his tone which made them listen uncomfortably.

It was not a long speech. It lasted only a minute or two. Then Opalo deliberately left his seat, skirted the checkered cloth before him, and stalked down the length of the building and out the door.

As soon as he was gone, the spell was broken. Somebody giggled, and there were smiles, pitying, tolerant, even a few that were scornful. But some of the faces of those who remained on the benches were grave, and some were angry, and a few a little fearful.

Chief Whitewater, who had not been able to understand what was said, was leaning past one of the musicians, receiving a translation from one of the elders. But Huck did not need a translation. He had understood, and he stood up, his black eyes apprehensive.

"Come on," he ordered. "We've got to go."

Not until he and the twins were safely outside, and away from listening ears, did he tell them why.

"Martha told my grandfather that one of the berry scouts ate a huckleberry before the proper ceremony. It was the message I was supposed to give him, but I didn't. I hoped he wouldn't find out. He says that the harvest gods have been insulted, so they've gone away. Terrible things can happen now. He's going to do what he can to ward off danger, and I know he'll head straight for the tepee."

"Then he'll find George," cried Joan. "And George will blame us."

"I don't care about that now," admitted Huck. "I just happened to think what it would do to my grandfather to see a real stegosaurus in his tepee. He's an old man. He might have a heart attack or something. We've got to stop it."

CHAPTER NINETEEN

"HERE HE COMES," said Joey. "He's finally started this way."

"Poor old man," pitied Joan. "He must have felt just terrible when he went to the place where he'd left his wigwam and all he found were his belongings scattered all over the grass. How could you have done that to him, George?"

"I don't see why you blame me." The buffalo hide twitched with the reptile's reproach. "If you own a movable cave, you have to expect it to move occasionally."

"I'd better go meet him," decided Huck. "I don't know exactly what to say, but——"

"Tell him to go away," ordered George nervously. "You promised to protect me, and I expect you to keep your promise."

Huck started wading through the tall grass. It caught in tangled lengths against his bare legs, impeding his progress. His promise to George had become of secondary importance now. He would have to warn his grandfather that under the buffalo hide was the strangest creature known to man, a creature that looked like a monster in one of his own visions. Opalo must be prepared. He couldn't be allowed to come face to face with a live dinosaur.

The old man had gone straight from the Longhouse

to where he had left his tepee, and Huck could imagine how he must have felt. Perhaps Opalo, too, had thought the poles had given way and that the tepee had tumbled into the grass. But when he arrived at the spot to find only pots and pans, clothes and bedding scattered in the grass, he had probably decided it had been stolen. When his dim eyes had finally sighted the familiar gray peak rising across the field behind the racetrack, what a shock it must have been. He couldn't have noticed it right away, either, for over an hour had passed since they left the Longhouse. Huck and his friends wanted to go looking for his grandfather, but George had grown nervous and now refused to be left alone. When they had started, he began to follow along, so there was nothing to do but go back and wait for Opalo to come to them.

The old man advanced slowly, his eyes on the deep growth through which he walked. Several times he stopped and kicked at something, bending low so he could see more closely. As Huck drew closer, he could see that Opalo was carrying objects important to his calling—a bone rattle, a small drum, and an old metal bell.

"Grandfather," he called as soon as he was close enough to be heard. "I want to tell you about your tepee. I didn't move it over there. There's——"

"You do not need to tell me that, boy." The black horsehair wig shook from side to side. "I know about the tepee. I know why it was moved, and how. And you must stay away from it, Weewino. You and your friends also. Even I, who have dealt with these things before, dare not go too close. The tepee is bewitched."

"Bewitched?"

"A spell has been put upon it," declared Opalo solemnly. "An evil spirit has taken possession of my grandfather's tepee. How else would it be able to stand upright without supports? The poles are scattered all through the grass."

"Maybe it's not an evil spirit," suggested Huck cautiously. "Maybe it's a live animal inside that's holding it up."

"You talk nonsense, boy," declared Opalo sharply. "No animal is larger than a buffalo, and my grandfather used the hides of more than one for his tepee." Again the horsehair flapped about the old face. "It is an evil spirit, and I know why it has come. One of the scouts ate of the berries before the proper ceremony. The harvest gods are angry, and they have turned from our people. So the evil spirit feels free to come, thinking that there is no one left to drive it away. But I am here, and I will do what must be done."

He stalked proudly past his grandson, to the rusty accompaniment of the iron bell in his hand, and Huck turned and followed. He had done the best he could. He had tried to suggest that the tepee wasn't being held up by supernatural forces, and Opalo wouldn't listen. But at least he wouldn't lift the flap and look inside. He meant to keep a respectful distance between himself and the buffalo skin.

As they drew close enough for the old man's eyes to pick out details, Opalo spoke over his shoulder.

"If you care about your friends, warn them of the

206

danger. They are standing so close that the evil spirit inside my grandfather's tepee could reach out and take them."

A little fearful lest George might take it in his head that the summons also included him, Huck raised his voice.

"Joey! Joan! Come here and walk back to the tepee with us."

As the twins obeyed, Huck observed that the old fence rails piled about the stegosaurus's tail teetered and moved in the grass but that the tepee itself remained motionless. He was glad that his grandfather hadn't noticed.

"Did you tell him?" Both Joey's and Joan's round blue eyes were anxious.

"He told me," said Huck significantly. "My grandfather knows how the tepee got moved. There's an evil spirit inside, and he's going to drive it away. Nobody must go close to the tepee, because that's dangerous. Even my grandfather must stay away from it."

"Drive it away?" repeated Joey in alarm. "He isn't going to shoot at it or anything?"

"The only way to drive away evil spirits is with noise," explained Huck. "They get tired of hearing it, or scared, and leave."

"Oh," said Joan in relief. Then she added thoughtfully, "That's a very good idea. Especially after it gets dark."

Opalo stopped a discreet twenty feet or so from where the tepee stood and began tromping down the grass with his feet. With a flip of the horsehair wig, he signified that Huck was to help in this endeavor, and the twins, anxious to be of service, joined in. The dry stalks snapped and bent under their feet, creating a little island in the high, waving field.

Although Huck had never seen anyone drive away an evil spirit, he had a general idea of how it would be done, for there were ceremonial dances which re-enacted this ancient ritual. Then he remembered that this wasn't a dance. This was the real thing. It was the old ceremony in which his forefathers used to believe, in which his grandfather still believed, and at which the younger generation of Indians scoffed. When the noise began—and there would be lots of noise, rattles and drums, bells and chanting—everyone would flock here from the Longhouse to stare. Some of them would

laugh. Nappy and Bob would laugh, and the other children from the school.

Perhaps even his friends, Joey and Joan, would finally come to laugh when they began to realize how futile and silly the whole thing was. Huck darted a quick glance at them now, wondering if they were already beginning to think it was funny. Joey's face was pink from the sun, and fresh freckles had popped out on his nose. He was stomping away at the tough grass as though his life depended upon beating it down. Catching Huck's eye, he asked eagerly, "Hey, who gets to beat the drum? Do you think maybe I could have a turn after a while?"

"I think so." Huck smiled, feeling better.

Joan stomped her way close to him and spoke softly in his ear.

"One of us ought to warn George not to get excited. He might start sharpening his tail."

"We can't," whispered Huck. "We don't dare go over there. We'll just have to keep our fingers crossed."

At last Opalo was satisfied with the flat circle in the grass. Apparently he accepted the children in the roles of assistants, for he motioned them to sit down on the ground. He handed the drum to Huck, the iron bell to Joey, and kept the bone rattle for himself.

"I didn't get anything, sir," Joan reminded him politely.

"You clap your hands," said Huck hastily. "The way the people did in the Longhouse."

Opalo advanced to the center of the ring, and for a long moment he stood glaring at the tepee rising out of the grass. He had stopped long enough at the original site to put fresh paint on his face, and when he brushed back the horsehair, they could see long blue streaks running down each cheek and that his old eyes stared out from blue-painted circles. He raised the bone rattle and shook it vengefully as he shrieked defiance to the evil spirit which had taken possession of his grandfather's tepee.

Huck began to beat on the drum, and Joey rang the bell as loudly as he could. Opalo began a chant similar to the one which had been sung in the Longhouse, and as he sang he danced. The old body bent almost double, then straightened for a few steps, while he shook the bone rattle high in the air. Around and around in a slow circle he went, and the charms on his thin arms and ankles rang with each high-lifted, short step. Huck joined his voice with his grandfather's, and after a moment Joan and Joey were able to pick up the simple, repetitious refrain.

Over in the corral, horses neighed, and before long people began drifting down from the Longhouse. By unspoken consent, they stopped by the fence corner, where they could peer down from a slight rise of ground at the solitary dancer and his musicians. The white visitors observed silently, and with polite smiles, thinking that this was part of the festival, although they whispered to each other that it was odd to see two red-haired white children taking part. But the Indians who came were not so restrained in their comments.

Huck heard someone calling his name, and when he raised up to peer over the grass tops, Chief Whitewater and Burt Franchere were standing a little ahead of the larger group.

"You beat the drum awhile," he said, thrusting it into Joan's willing hands. Opalo had not slowed in his dance at the interruption. Perhaps he had not heard. "I'll be right back."

"Just what's going on here, Huck?" demanded the chief as he reached the fence. "Your grandfather's liable to bring on a stroke. He's too old to carry on that way."

"He's driving out an evil spirit, sir," said Huck unhappily. "It's in his tepee."

"Well, something's certainly wrong with that tepee." Chief Whitewater frowned, squinting into the sun. "Who put it up, anyway?"

"Jack and I helped put it up last night," said Burt Franchere quickly. "But it wasn't here, and it didn't look like that when we were through. Somebody moved it since. Did you find out who, Huck?"

"Grandfather says an evil spirit moved it."

"Somebody's playing tricks on the old man." The chief frowned. "And I don't like it. They've got it rigged up on some kind of a frame. There's no center poles coming out of the top. Come on, Burt. Let's go have a look."

"No. Please!" Huck grabbed the chief's leather sleeve in both hands, holding him back. "Grandfather says no one is to go near it. Nobody."

"If Opalo, medicine man of the Klickitats, says that everyone must stay away, that is the way it will be. And even if you are the chief, you will do as he says. It is his tepee, and he has the right to say who may enter."

Old Martha had come up behind them on silent, moccasined feet. In the sunlight, her eyes glittered like thin black stones.

"You shouldn't be out here, Grandmother." Chief Whitewater turned in dismay. "You ought to be taking it easy."

"How can anyone take things easy when trouble is coming to our people?" she asked scornfully. "The old ways have been broken."

"I know. I know. Florence Bigsaw ate a huckleberry before it was time," he agreed helplessly. "But it was only one little berry."

"One berry, one evil spirit," she reminded him darkly. "Opalo tries to drive it away before it has done harm."

"He'll have a heart attack, Grandmother. He'll kill himself carrying on that way."

"What must be must be," she shrugged. "Opalo does as he should."

"I don't think you can stop him, Charley," said Burt Franchere. "He's doing what he thinks is right, just as your grandmother says. If you kept him from what he considered his duty, it would break his heart. And the older ones in the tribe would never forgive you. He'll tire himself out pretty soon and have to stop."

"And I suppose you agree that we ought to stay away from that misshapen joke of a tepee, too," said Chief Whitewater bitterly. "You think a man's home is his castle, I suppose?"

"Well, it's his." Burt nodded. "He doesn't want anyone out there, and he ought to be able to say."

"All right." The chief gave in with a shrug of his beaded shoulders. "Huck, try to get him to lay off when it looks like he's getting winded, will you? The rodeo's about ready to start, and I'm expected to be there. Grandmother, shall I help you back to the Longhouse first?"

"Help yourself back," she snapped. "I will stay here until Opalo drives out the bad spirit."

Huck returned to the others with mingled emotions. He was glad that Martha was going to remain, for she would keep everyone away from the tepee. She would tell them that it was by the chief's orders that they must keep their distance, and no one would dispute that. But Huck hadn't considered the possibility that this strenuous exercise might be a strain on his grandfather. He looked at the old man carefully as he squatted down on the ground, clapping his hands in time with the drum, since he knew that Joan would not want to relinquish it so soon. Opalo gave no indication of suffering from a weak heart. He lifted his heels as high as ever, and his voice was steady in its chanted threats against wayward spirits.

The crowd of spectators dwindled after the rodeo began. Only a few of the older Indians like Martha, staunch believers in the thing that Opalo was trying to do, remained silently watching in the background.

They could hear sounds from the track, pounding hoofs, screaming spectators, the mighty thud as a Brahma bull tumbled in the dust, but these were undertones to their own chanting and to the ringing bell, the pounding drum. All the children were growing hoarse by this time. Their voices came out in rough croaks, and by mutual consent they took turns resting. Only Opalo's chant was as steady as when he had begun in the early afternoon.

They could tell when the rodeo ended and the Indian wrestling began, because someone announced it through a megaphone, but they could not see what was going on, surrounded as they were by waving grasses which reached above their heads. Huck remembered that this was the part which had lured George from his solitude. He hoped the stegosaurus would not be disappointed.

By the time the last event was over, the sun had sunk below the line of trees along the river and the sky was growing pink. Joey and Joan had long since stopped trying to keep up with the chant, and even Huck was able to croak only an occasional note or two. But they continued to beat the drum, ring the bell, and clap tired palm against tired palm as an accompaniment to Opalo's apparently tireless dance. Huck didn't see how his grandfather could keep on. They had eaten breakfast with the Francheres, but their noon meal had been only the traditional first tastes. His own stomach ached painfully.

A crowd had rejoined the faithful spectators by the fence after the Indian wrestling, and it was a different crowd from the one before. These were the scoffers. Huck could hear them laughing and making cruel remarks. He clenched his teeth tightly together, but he could not close his ears. Then he heard a woman's voice calling the twins.

"Joey! Joan! Your aunt said to have you at the parking lot at seven-thirty. You kids come on now."

"It's Mildred," said Joan hoarsely, looking at her brother. "What'll we do?"

"We can't walk out on them now. Not till it gets dark and we make sure George gets away," said Joey, and Huck's heart gave a happy thump at his friend's loyalty. "You go tell Mildred we can't come yet. Ask Auntie Casey to wait. Oh, and tell Mildred to get those bananas out of the trunk for Huck's grandfather. We don't want to forget them again."

Joan nodded and got up stiffly. Her head, appearing out of the grass, was greeted by hooting jeers from the spectators, but she didn't seem to mind. Huck saw her toss her red pigtails defiantly before she waded away in the direction of the fence.

She was gone for some time, and when she returned, her sunburned face was even pinker with indignation.

"She sure is mad," she told Huck and Joey. "She says she's going to tell Auntie Casey all kinds of things —about how bad we were and how we ran off and wouldn't mind her. She's gone up to the parking lot to wait for her now."

"Maybe you ought to go," suggested Huck miserably. "I don't want you to get in trouble on my account."

"No, sir." Joey frowned. "We're staying. It'll be dark pretty soon."

"It doesn't even have to be clear dark. Just pretty dark," said Joan. "Anyway, a lot of the cars are already gone from the field, so it will be safer for George to walk along the road."

That was a comforting thought to all of them. George had followed the road to get here, and he would probably need to retrace his steps to find his way home. He wouldn't be able to make time if he had to keep ducking off to one side to avoid the lights of passing cars.

"Why don't you sit down?" demanded Joey, tilting his head to look up at his sister.

"It feels good to stand up," she told him. "We've been sitting all afternoon. You ought to try it."

"I will, if I can stand on my foot," said Joey doubtfully. "It's gone to sleep."

He missed a few drumbeats getting up, but Opalo, still bending and raising, chanting and shaking his bone rattle, gave no indication that he noticed. The old man seemed tireless.

A fresh burst of laughter from those by the fence greeted the appearance of Joey's head and upper body above the grass. It made Huck grate his teeth in anger, and he, too, stood up, ringing the iron bell as loudly as he could.

"Want me to help you call the monster, Huck? I'm good at it."

Although he did not turn, he recognized Nappy's voice as it floated down the slight rise. Let them laugh, he thought angrily. It didn't matter. But someday he'd show them. Someday they'd be sorry.

Deliberately he tried to make himself think of other things. How was George getting along out there in the field? It must be uncomfortably warm under the buffalo hide. Was he getting as tired of standing up as they had grown of sitting? And what a strain it must have been not to sharpen his tail. The wind was blowing down the slope, and the scent of men always made the stegosaurus nervous.

Huck looked across the grass tops at his grandfather's tepee, silhouetted against the evening sky. It hardly looked like a tepee at all. It looked exactly like what it was—a stegosaurus hiding under buffalo skins. Fortunately, most people wouldn't think of that, for they had never seen a stegosaurus. In the gathering twilight, the tepee looked farther away than it had before—or had George, in his uneasiness, been inching backward through the grass?

Huck was pleased that night was coming on so swiftly. He could smell it in the air. There were the scents of the day's sun fading from the grass, of the river beyond the trees, of horses in the corral, and of smoke from the cooking fires, started now in the tepee city. And then his nostrils quivered, for he smelled something else, a sweetish smell that was familiar and yet did not belong here. The wind was blowing it down the little rise, and it seemed to be growing stronger by the minute.

"Joey Brown! Joan Brown!" Mildred's voice, bristling with new authority, rose above the laughing murmur behind them. "Your aunt says you're to stop making a spectacle of yourself and come this minute. Her feet's too tired to walk here herself, but she says you're to mind me and I'm to bring you to the car."

Huck turned to see Mildred Post wading through the grass toward them. The others, possibly because of Martha's orders, had continued to observe from a distance, but Mildred no longer felt that she needed to obey those restrictions. She had been sent to fetch the Brown children, and she intended to do so, even if she had to drag them. Huck could now see the cause of the familiar sweetish odor, for Mildred's extended arm held high a skinny stalk, at the bottom of which clustered a mass of soft, brown, overripe bananas.

For the first time, Opalo faltered in his dance. The rattle dropped to his side, and glazed eyes, within painted blue circles, turned toward the approaching woman.

"Mrs. Casey said to bring these along," she called, disdainfully holding the stalk away from her. "She says they're spoiled from being all day in that hot trunk, but that you'd want to see for yourself, most likely. Phew! They sure do smell!"

"Our bananas!" cried Joan in dismay. "They were a present for your grandfather, Huck."

"Give them to him anyway," chuckled Mildred, coming up to the circle. "They say it's the thought that counts, not the present."

Her voice broke off in a scream, and she jerked back an empty hand, which only a moment before had been holding a banana stalk, as though it had been burned.

Huck staggered to keep his footing as something rough and hard and leathery almost pushed him from his feet. It came between him and the twins like a huge, dark cloud, and something long, with a knobby round end, thrust out from the larger mass to snatch the odorous banana stalk from Mildred's hand. He could hear her screaming again and again, as though she would never stop; then the dark mass drew back, letting him see Joey's and Joan's open mouths and staring, startled eyes.

"Begone! Begone! Never threaten our people again!" shrieked Opalo in Klickitat, and the bone rattle shook menacingly after his grandfather's tepee, which was galloping away through the grass toward the sheltering trees along the river.

"Somebody better catch it," called a nervous voice from the now silent spectators. "There's somebody inside that tepee. A thief!"

"No!" Opalo's voice rang out. He spoke in English, but no one seemed aware of the fact. "You cannot catch an evil spirit. Let it go."

They obeyed him without question, continuing to stand, speaking in nervous undertones until the dark shape had been swallowed up by the twilight. Then Opalo spoke in Klickitat to his grandson, and his voice was old and petulant.

"Tell that woman to be silent!"

Mildred was crying hysterically, repeating over and over that her life had been threatened, that something had tried to gobble her up.

"My grandfather says to be quiet," Huck ordered disdainfully. "He says if you don't, he'll call the evil spirit back, and this time it will really get you."

Mildred's sobs silenced immediately.

"Please don't let him do that," she gasped. "I wouldn't want that to happen. Ever again."

CHAPTER *TWENTY*

"Is it all right
if I go to see my friends?" Huck asked when they had
finished their morning meal. "I could do the washing
at the hot spring on the way."

His grandfather nodded silent permission before he
crossed the room and stood a moment in the open doorway. Opalo had not said much this morning, but the
thoughts which occupied his mind could not have
been unpleasant, for his features were relaxed and the
old eyes held a glint of satisfaction.

They had both been weary when they reached home,
long after dark, the night before. The Huckleberry Festival had been brought to an early close by a heavy
rainstorm, which continued throughout Monday. The
tepee village grew sodden and uncomfortable. Fires
smoked and sputtered out. The racetrack melted into
a slippery circle of mud, and the old men, who sat in
the Longhouse, repeating the ancient stories, grew tired
of straining their voices to compete with the steady
downpour on the low roof.

By early afternoon, everyone was packed up and on
his way home. Opalo had received more than one offer
of a ride. People like Chief Whitewater and Burt
Franchere were thinking that the long, wet hours in
a horse-drawn wagon could be reduced to quick com-
fort in a closed car. Others, like the Posts, had been

moved by uneasy remembrance of a tepee galloping out of the grass to snatch a stalk of overripe bananas from Mildred's hand. Now that they had time to consider it carefully, they told one another that it must have been a trick but that anyone who could execute such illusions was worthy of respect. Besides, they couldn't be sure. The old ones held medicine men in veneration, and there had to be some reason behind that.

Opalo had declined all invitations. He and his grandson had come in the wagon; they would return the same way. The buffalo hide, which had been discovered Sunday morning alongside the road a mile beyond the tepee village, was bundled into the back, and they had started out. Only once had they held a brief conversation en route.

"Are you sure you want to stay with the Francheres, Grandfather?" Huck had asked anxiously.

It had seemed like a miracle when Burt made the offer, and he had held his breath until Opalo accepted. Burt had not known that there were plans to move the old man from his acres, or he would have offered before. His older children were married, Lily would be away at college, and there was only Jack at home. There was plenty of room, and he did not think that Opalo would be happy at the Posts'.

"It is not right that a medicine man do a squaw's work." His grandfather had to lift his voice to carry above the splash of rain and the plodding thumps of Paint's unshod feet on the wet road. "And it is no longer right that you should do so, either, Weewino.

Soon you will be a young brave and will have work of your own."

"But next summer, when school is out, we'll both go home," Huck reminded him. "I won't mind doing it then, Grandfather. We'll be together every summer."

"And someday you will have a squaw of your own." Opalo nodded. "Then we will be together always. Until that time I will spend my winters with Burt Franchere. He is a good man, and his squaw is a good cook. Besides, he asks my help. The young chief has come to his senses. The children will be taught the tongue of their fathers before it is forgotten. The chief himself will join the class which Burt Franchere will instruct. He needs me to advise him."

The old man fell silent, but his tired eyes, under the wide-brimmed felt hat which poured two constant streams of water onto his coat, were proud. He had reason for pride, Huck remembered. At the insistence of Chief Whitewater, Opalo had finally submitted to a checkup by Dr. Mercer at the conclusion of the long dance to drive out the evil spirit. The doctor could hardly believe his stethoscope. The old man's heartbeat was a little fast, but it was strong and steady and would have done credit to a man half his age.

Now Huck gathered the soiled clothing into a bundle and went outside. His grandfather was sitting on an upturned log. The morning sun picked out every wrinkle in his leathery face, and he looked very thin and old. Then he looked up and smiled, and he didn't look very old at all.

"Go to your friends," he said. "They are good children. They tried to help when we needed them. Give them the thanks of Opalo for what they did. I will be here when you return."

Although sun had replaced yesterday's rain, the storm had left noticeable effects. The clouds had rolled away to leave a paler blue in the sky. The dry earth had absorbed the moisture, but the caked dust in the road no longer rose in saffron swirls under Huck's moccasins. There was the first smell of fall in the air, and when he looked up, at a faraway honking, he saw a black V in the sky, which moved swiftly out of sight. It was the first flight of geese, and it was earlier than usual for them to fly south. Perhaps they meant an early winter.

As he approached the spur of rock concealing the hot spring, he could hear voices, and when he rounded the tip he saw that the twins had come calling on George.

The stegosaurus was not his usual cheery self today. His head hung lower than ever, and although his eyes were open, they looked blankly dull and gave the appearance of seeing nothing. Even the spiked tail was motionless. It dragged behind the great, humped body and bore fresh traces of mud, for the sun had not yet found its way into the rocky enclosure.

"Hi." Joey beamed, breaking off what Huck imagined must have been a lecture directed to George.

"Hi," said Joan. There was a covered basket at her feet, which could contain a picnic lunch. Huck hoped that it did.

"Hi," he answered. "Hello, George."

"Hello," said George in a strangely weak voice. Then

his mouth opened hugely in a pink yawn which showed all his teeth and a long, curving tongue.

"We woke him up," explained Joan. "He's been asleep."

"The rains began, didn't they?" mumbled George.

"But they've stopped now," Joey pointed out impatiently. "The sun's shining. And it's our last day here, and we've brought a picnic. Now all you want to do is sleep."

"Your last day?" cried Huck, and a hard little ball seemed to form in his stomach.

"We've got to go home." Joan nodded. "A letter came Saturday. Mother and the professor are back. We're supposed to leave tomorrow."

"Tomorrow," mumbled George vaguely. "When the sun shines tomorrow, I will awaken."

Joan patted him gently on the nose.

"But that will be too late, George. We'll be gone. You won't see us—maybe ever again."

"Don't talk that way." Joey frowned. "We'll be back to visit next summer. Auntie Casey said so."

"I wish you didn't have to go," said Huck miserably. "I wish you could stay till school opens, anyway. That's only a couple of weeks away."

"That's why we have to go," explained Joan sadly. "To get ready for school."

"Will you look at that!" said Joey indignantly. "George is asleep again."

"His eyes are still open," objected Huck.

"That's because he hasn't any eyelids. But he's asleep, all right. He doesn't even know we're here."

"Was he like that when you first came?" Huck asked.

"He wasn't here at all when we came. At least we didn't see him. We called and called for a long time before he heard us and came down the side of the cliff."

"We were afraid that he'd gone away for good," Joan confessed. "After all, we hadn't seen him since the Huckleberry Festival, and that must have been awfully scary for him. There were lots of people, and even though they couldn't see him under the tepee, they probably made him very nervous."

"I'm glad he came, though," admitted Huck. "Nappy and Bob will never play medicine man again, not after they saw that tepee coming straight at them."

"Mildred says you and Nappy are best friends now," said Joan slyly. "And she's terribly disappointed that your grandfather isn't going to stay with them next winter."

"I don't think we'll ever be best friends." Huck grinned. "But he won't make any more trouble for me. He's scared of my grandfather."

"It was a swell festival," remembered Joey. "What we got to see of it. Maybe when we come to visit Auntie Casey next summer, you'll be having another, but we'd better not tell George about it."

"I'm sorry about the bananas, though," said Joan. "They were meant for your grandfather."

"I don't think he minded, really," said Huck, beginning to unwrap his bundle of laundry. "I think he expected the evil spirit to take something before it went away."

When the twins understood about the laundry, they offered to help. They had never heard of washing clothes in a mineral spring, and they declared that the results were far superior to automatic washing machines.

"And cheaper, too," declared Joey. "You don't even need soap."

By the time the clothes were spread out on juniper bushes to dry, everyone was ready for lunch. It would have been pleasanter had they found a sunny spot along the ledge, but it didn't seem right to leave George alone too long, so Joan spread the contents of the picnic basket on a large boulder close to the hot spring.

The sun was just beginning to find its way over the rimrock. It coaxed tiny wisps of steam from ground still damp from yesterday's downpour and glittered in little pools which had been caught in hollowed rocks. As they began on their sandwiches, the first rays fell on the tail of the stegosaurus, trailing motionless in the mud.

"It's kind of cold in here, isn't it?" Joan shivered, biting into a tuna fish sandwich. She had carefully segregated them before anyone started eating, putting aside the three made of cheese for their vegetarian friend. "Maybe it's just as well we're going home. Summer's almost over."

"We could still have a long fall," declared Joey. "This is just the first rain. It doesn't mean anything, does it, Huck?"

"I don't know." Huck shook his head doubtfully, remembering the geese he had seen that morning. "But I hate to think of winter. What do you suppose will happen to George?"

"If you and your grandfather aren't there, he could stay in your house," suggested Joan.

"He couldn't get in the door."

"He's got a cave somewhere," said Joey. "That's probably where he stays in the winter."

"But what does he eat? The snow gets pretty deep up here sometimes. The sagebrush is covered up."

"Maybe he lays in a supply ahead of time," said Joan, but her tone suggested that she did not really think George was so farsighted.

They turned and looked at their friend, standing motionless on four great legs, so like gnarled stumps of mighty trees. The sun had crept higher, until he was now entirely bathed in light, and as they watched a quiver ran down the length of the plated back. It began with his nose and ended with his tail, raising it from the mud and starting it to wag back and forth in the friendly pendulum motion they knew so well. The head raised, the film vanished from across the beady eyes, and the next moment George advanced happily toward them.

"My dear friends! This is a pleasure. You have come to call and brought a picnic."

"We've been here a long time," said Joey pointedly. "You wouldn't wake up."

"Ah, but it was still chilly after the rain," George reminded him. "When it is cold, my instinct says to sleep. When it is warm, it tells me to awaken. But I cannot imagine how I came to be standing here in the open."

"You came because you heard us calling you, George,"

said Joan gently. "But I don't think you were clear awake, even then."

"Probably not," declared the stegosaurus, eyeing the lunch on the boulder. "I don't suppose you brought any bananas?"

Joan hurried to offer him one of the sandwiches.

"I'm afraid not. You saw what happened to the last ones. They spoiled before anyone could eat them."

George choked a little on the cheese.

"You can't mean the ones that were served at the picnic? Why, those were exactly the way I like them. Fully ripe. Without them, I would have had to call that picnic a flop. All those mammals. And that dreadful noise. Even the Indian wrestling was inferior. I could have beaten any of the contestants without half trying. But when the refreshments were passed, they made up for everything. I'm glad you invited me."

"And I'm glad you came, George," said Huck earnestly. "I don't know what I'd have done without you."

"Neither do I," agreed George. The beady eyes regarded Huck anxiously for a minute; then he turned to the twins. "It worries me to think what our poor friend will do during the cold time that is coming. You must promise to look after him."

"The cold time?" repeated Joan. "Do you mean winter, George?"

"What is winter?" asked the stegosaurus courteously.

"It's the time of year when snow is on the ground," explained Huck, trying not to resent the inference that he was incapable of taking care of himself.

"And what is snow?"

"It's that cold, white stuff that covers the ground. Even the sagebrush."

"Poor, dear, stupid mammal," sighed George, between gulps of bread and cheese. "What an imagination! Where could he have got such an idea? Cold, white stuff covering all the ground. Even the sagebrush. And he actually believes it!"

"Haven't you ever seen snow, George?" asked Joan.

"You mustn't encourage him in those flights of fancy, Joan," he told her severely. "You and I know there is no such phenomenon. I have been here millions of years, and if there were, I would have seen it. There is a cold time and a warm time, nothing more."

"Where are you in the winter—in the cold time?" asked Joey cautiously.

"Asleep, naturally," George told him. "There are always a few warnings, short naps, which give me time to fill my stomach in preparation for the real sleep. Then the cold time begins, and I go to my cave and sleep until it has gone away."

"He hibernates!" cried Joey. "That's what happens to George in the winter. We don't have to worry at all."

"It's my instinct," said George smugly. "But our dear friend has not yet developed his. How will he manage through the cold time?"

"He'll be fine," promised Joey. "He'll be in school. That's in a heated building, and men store up food, so there's plenty to eat. We'll all be in school. It's a place where children go to learn things."

"Perhaps that is why I have never been able to develop my brain. I have never been to school," said

George sadly. He had been about to take a peach from the picnic cloth on top of the boulder, but suddenly he drew back and his black eyes stared at the children, each in turn.

"You are going away!" he accused. "You're going away to this school. Your brain development is more important to you than our friendship. You are leaving me alone."

"But we have to go," argued Joey. "And it's only for a few months. Huck will be back here to live next summer, and Joan and I will come to visit then."

"What is summer?" demanded the stegosaurus sulkily.

"That's when it gets hot," explained Joan. "Winter's the cold months. Summer's the hot ones."

Suddenly the stegosaurus began to laugh. They had never heard him laugh before, and the sound, which had the squeaking qualities of someone sharpening a rusty saw, made them jump in mild alarm.

"Oh, for goodness' sake," declared George, when he was finally able to restrain himself. "For a minute, I thought you were serious about leaving me. I didn't know you were only joking. You'll all be here when I wake up. I won't even have time to miss you."

D31